Anonymous

The prescriber's epitome of the British pharmacopoeia of 1867

SALZWASSER
VERLAG

Anonymous

The prescriber's epitome of the British pharmacopoeia of 1867

1st Edition | ISBN: 978-3-75250-494-1

Place of Publication: Frankfurt am Main, Germany

Year of Publication: 2020

Salzwasser Verlag GmbH, Germany.

Reprint of the original, first published in 1869.

THE

PRESCRIBER'S EPITOME

OF THE

BRITISH PHARMACOPŒIA

OF

1 8 6 7.

———————

BY A SURGEON.

———————

LONDON:

PUBLISHED BY H. SILVERLOCK

17, EARL STREET, DOCTORS' COMMONS, E.C
AND
92, BLACKFRIARS ROAD, S.E.

———

MDCCCLXIX.

PREFACE.

HE vicissitudes through which *Materia Medica* and Medinal Compounds had to pass in the process of amalgamating
e Pharmacopœias of London, Edinburgh, and Dublin, have
ecessarily produced some amount of confusion as to the
ature and strength of old and new formulæ.

To meet this difficulty this Epitome is written; and as
is especially compiled for the use of Prescribers, any notice
f the Appendix of the British Pharmacopœia is omitted, as
eing foreign to the purpose, except so far as weights and
easures are concerned—the old symbols for ounce, drachm,
nd scruple being retained.

The nomenclature has been carefully abbreviated to an
xtent convenient in prescribing, without, it is hoped,
nning any risk of confounding one substance or compound
ith another.

The Compiler is indebted in most instances to the works
f PEREIRA, GARROD, ROYLE, and other authorities, for the
utlines of the properties and uses of the various Drugs and
reparations as far as they are given.

A 2

The Compounds into which any particular substance enters, or its proportions in the same, are in most instances indicated.

Those substances which are only employed in the preparation of other Compounds are marked *.

All Tinctures marked (s.r.) are made with Rectified Spirit.

When the dose is *not* on the authority of the British Pharmacopœia it is placed last of all.

The more doubtful Properties of the Drugs are marked (?).

A. G. B.

London, 1869.

THE
PRESCRIBER'S EPITOME

OF THE

BRITISH PHARMACOPŒIA.

*ACACIA GUMMI.
Mucilaginous Demul.

ACETUM. (D. fl. ℨj—ij.)
(*Vide* Acid: Acetic: Dil:)

ACETUM CANTHARID:
Ext: Rubefacient, Epispastic.

ACETUM SCILLÆ. (D. m. 15—40.)
Expectorant and Diuretic.

ACID: ACETIC:
Vesicant and Escharotic.

ACID: ACETIC: DIL: (D. fl. ℨj—ij.)
Cooling Lotion.
The vapour in Throat and Laryngeal Affections.

ACID: ACETIC: GLACIAL:
Caustic Irritant, Vesicant, and Escharotic.
Warts, Corns, &c.

ACID: ARSENIOSUM. (D. gr. $\frac{1}{60}$—$\frac{1}{12}$ in solution.)
LIQ: ARSENICALIS, contains grs. 4 in fl. ℨj.
LIQ: ARSENICI HYDROCHLOR: contains grs. 4 in fl. ℨj.
Caustic, Alterative.
Agues, Neuralgia, Lepra, Chorea, Vesicular and Pustular Eruptions, Cancer.

ACID: BENZOIC: (D. gr. 10—15.)
Stimulant, Expectorant.
The Kidneys secrete it as Hippuric Acid.

A 3

ACID: CARBOLIC: (D. gr. 1—8.)
  Powerful Antiseptic; Internally, acts like Creasote.
  Gangrenous and Fœtid Sores, Necrosis, Caries.

ACID: CITRIC: (D. gr. 10—80.)
  Refrigerant, Febrifuge.
  Allays Thirst and Irritation of Skin.

ACID: GALLIC: (D. gr. 2—10.)
  EXT: Less Astringent than Tannic Acid, but
  INT: Rather more so.
  Hæmorrhages, Gleet, Leucorrhœa.

*ACID: HYDROCHLOR:

ACID: HYDROCHLOR: DIL: (D. m. 10—80.)
  Alterative, Tonic, Refrigerant, and Astringent.

ACID: HYDROCYAN: DIL: (D. m. 2—8.)
  Poisonous—General Anodyne and Sedative.
  Gastrodynia, Pyrosis, Asthma.

ACID: NITRIC:
  Caustic.
  Phagedenic Sores.

ACID: NITRIC: DIL: (D. m. 10—80.)
  Refrigerant, Tonic, and Alterative.
  Solvent for Phosphatic Calculi.
  Scrofulous and Syphilitic Affections.

ACID: NITRO-HYDROCHLOR: DIL: (D. m. 5—20.)
  EXT: Powerful Caustic and Acrid Poison.
  INT: When diluted, Refrigerant, Tonic, and Astringent.

ACID: PHOSPH: DIL: (D. m. 10—80.)
  Stimulant, Refrigerant.
  Alkaline Urine, Ossification of Arteries, Caries, Mollities
  Osseum; allays Thirst in Diabetes, &c.

*ACID: SULPHURIC:

ACID: SULPH: AROMAT: (D. m. 5—80.)
  An agreeable form for exhibiting Sulphuric Acid.

ACID: SULPH: DIL: (D. m. 5—80.)
  Refrigerant, Tonic, Astringent.
  Allays Thirst in Hectic, &c., checks Sweating in Phthisis.
  Hæmorrhagic Diathesis.

ACID: SULPHUROSUM. (D. fl. ʒꜱ—j.)
EXT: Skin Affections dependant on Vegetations, *e.g.* Porrigo.

ACID: TANNIC: (D. gr. 2—10.)
Powerful Astringent.
Kidneys secrete it as Gallic and Pyrogallic Acids.
Hæmorrhages, Hectic Sweating, Diarrhœa, Gleet, Leucorrhœa.

ACID: TARTARIC: (D. gr. 10—80.)
Refrigerant in Fevers.

*ACONITI FOLIA.
Vide Ext: Aconiti.

*ACONITI RADIX.
Vide Linim: and Tinct: Aconiti.

*ACONITIA.
Vide Linim: Tinct: and Ext: Aconiti

ADEPS BENZOATUS.
A stimulating basis for Suppositories and Ointments.

AOEPS PRÆPARAT:
Oleaginous Demulcent, Emollient

ÆTHER. (D. m. 20—60.)
INT: Diffusible Stimulant, Antispasmodic.
Spasmodic Asthma, Angina Pectoris, Hysteria.
EXT: Refrigerant.

*ÆTHER PURUS.

ALBUMEN OVI.
Antidote in Poisoning by Corrosive Sublimate and Sulphate of Copper.

*ALCOHOL AMYLIC:

ALOE: BARB: (D. gr. 2—6.)
Vide Aloe: Soc:
Preparations:—
ENEMA ALOE: 4 grs. in fl. ʒj.
EXT: ALOE: BARB: 8 parts from 10, nearly.
PIL: ALOE: BARB: 1 part in 2, nearly.
PIL: ALOE: ET FERRI, 1 part in 5¼.
PIL: CAMBOG: Co: 1 part in 6, nearly.
PIL: COLOCYNTH: Co: 1 part in 8, nearly.
PIL: COLOCYNTH: ET HYOSCYAM: 1 part in 4½, nearly.

ALOE: SOC: (D. gr. 2—6.)

Purgative, (specially acting on lower part of Intestinal Canal,) Emmenagogue, Tonic and Stomachic in small doses.

In Habitual Constipation.

Preparations:—

DECOCT: ALOE : Co: 4 grs. Ext: in fl. ℥j.
ENEMA ALOE : 4 gr. in fl. ℥j.
EXT: ALOE: SOC: 1 part from 2, nearly.
EXT: COLOCYNTH: Co: 1 part Ext: in 2¼, nearly.
PIL: ALOE: ET ASSAFŒT: 1 part in 4.
PIL: ALOE: ET MYRRH: 1 part in 8.
PIL: ALOE: SOC: 1 part in 2, nearly.
PIL: RHEI Co: 1 part in 6.
TINCT: ALOE: 11 grs. to fl. ℥j.
TINCT: BENZOIN : Co: 8 grs. to fl. ℥j.
VIN: ALOE : 16½ grs. to fl. ℥j.

ALUMEN. (D. gr. 10—20.)

Astringent ; in large doses, Purgative.

Sore Throat, Leucorrhœa, Hooping Cough, Hæmorrhages.

ALUMEN EXSIC:

Slight Escharotic.

AMMONIACUM.

Less Antispasmodic than Assafœtida, but more Expectorant.

Chronic Bronchitis.　　　　　　　　　　　•

AMMON: BENZOAS. (D. gr. 10—20.)

Diuretic and slightly Stimulant.

Chronic Inf am: of Bladder, Phosphatic Deposits.

AMMON: CARB: (D. gr. 8—10.)

20 grs. neutralize { 23½ grs. Citric Acid.
                     25½ Tartaric Acid.

Vide Liq: Ammoniæ.

AMMON: PHOSPH: (D. gr. 5—20.)

Solvent in Uric Acid Calculi.

Gouty Diathesis.

AMMON: BROMID: (D. gr. 2—20.)

Acts as Potass: Bromid:

Hooping Cough, Epilepsy.

AMMON: CHLOR: (D. gr. 5—20.)

Increases the Secretions generally.

Neuralgia, Chronic Rheumatism, Inflam: Affections.

*AMYGD: AMARA.
    Contains Prussic Acid.

*AMYGD: DULC:
    Nutritive Demulcent.

AMYLUM.
    Amylaceous Demulcent.
        EXT: Some forms of Skin disease.

*ANETHI FRUCT.

ANTHEM: FLOR:
    Vide Ext: Infus: and Ol: Anthem:
    Sometimes used for Poultices.

ANTIM: OXIO: (D. gr. 1—4.)
    PULV: ANTIM: contains 1 part in 8.
    Diaphoretic and slightly Alterative.
        (Not so active as Tartar Emetic.)

*ANTIM: NIG:

ANTIM: SULPHURAT: (D. gr. 1—5.)
    PIL: HYDRARG: SUBCHLOR: Co: contains 1 part in 5.
    Action same as Antim : Tartarat:

ANTIM: TARTARAT: $\begin{cases} \text{D.} & \text{(Diaphoretic, gr. } \frac{1}{16}-\frac{1}{6}.) \\ & \text{(Emetic, gr. 1—2.)} \end{cases}$
    UNGT: ANTIM: TARTARAT: contains 1 part in 5.
    VIN: ANTIM: contains gr. 2 in fl. $\bar{3}$j.
    Vascular Depressant, or Sedative, in doses of gr. $\frac{1}{8}$ to 2.

AQUA.
    Diluent.

AQ: ANETHI.
    Stimulant, Aromatic, Carminative.
    Flatulency in Infants.

AQ: AUR: FLOR:
    Vehicle for flavour.

AQ: CAMPH: (D. fl. $\bar{3}$j—ij.)
    EXT: Stimulant, Calmative in Mania, Melancholy.
    INT: Stimulant, and afterwards Sedative, Antispasmodic,
    Diaphoretic.
        Dysmenorrhœa, Rheumatism.

AQ: CARUI.
    Aromatic, Stomachic, Carminative.
    Corrects Flatulence.

AQ: CINNAM:
Stimulant, Aromatic, Carminative, slightly Astringent.

AQ: DEST:

AQ: FŒNICULI.
Stimulant, Aromatic, Carminative.
Flatulence, Griping.

AQ: LAUROCERASI. (D. m. 5—30.)
Action, same as Prussic Acid, but of uncertain strength.

AQ: MENTH: PIP:
Stimulant, Carminative.
Corrects Flatulency.

AQ: MENTH: VIR:
Stimulant, Carminative.
Corrects Flatulency.

AQ: PIMENTÆ.
Stimulant, Aromatic, Carminative.
Atonic Dyspepsia, Vomiting in Pregnancy, Flatulence.

AQ: ROSÆ.
An agreeable vehicle.

AQ: SAMBUCI. (D. fl. ʒj—ij.)
Gently Stimulant.

ARGENT: NIT: (D. gr. $\frac{1}{8}$—$\frac{1}{2}$.)
Ext: Astringent, Irritant, Vesicant, Escharotic.
Int: Astringent, Alterative, Tonic.
Reduced to Oxide by light acting on the Skin, and so permanently discolouring it.

ARGENT: OXID: (D. gr. $\frac{1}{4}$—2.)
Int: Same as Argent: Nit:

*ARGENT: PURIF:

*ARMORACIÆ RAD:

*ARNICÆ RAD:

ASSAFŒTIDA. (D. gr. 5—20.)
Preparations:—
Enema Assafœt: gr. 30 to fl. ʒiv.
Pil: Aloe: et Assafœt: 1 part in 4.
Pil: Assafœt: Co: 1 part in 8½.
Spr: Ammon: Fœtid: gr. 38 to fl. ʒj.
Tinct: Assafœt: gr. 54½ to fl. ʒj.
Stimulant, Powerful Antispasmodic, Expectorant.
In Hysteria, Pertussis, Asthma, Bronchitis.

ATROPIA.
ATROPIÆ LIQ: gr. 4 in fl. ℥j.
,,   SULPH: LIQ: gr. 4 in fl. ℥j.
,,   UNG: gr. 8 in fl. ℥j.

+ATROPIÆ SULPH:
LIQ: ATROPIÆ SULPH: gr. 4 in fl. ℥j.
Topically it dilates Pupil, also allays pain.
Often used Hypodermically.

*AURANTII CORT:
BALS: PERU: (D. m. 10—15.)
Stimulant, Expectorant, Controls Excessive Discharges.
Bed Sores, Unhealthy Ulcers.

BALS: TOLUT: (D. grs. 10—20.)
Same as Bals: Peru:

BEBERIÆ SULPH: (D. gr. 1—10.)
Tonic, Antiperiodic.
(Inferior to Quinine.)

*BELÆ FRUCT:
*BELLADON: FOL:
Preparations:— { EXT: BELLADON:
TINCT: BELLADON:

*BELLADON: RAD:
Preparations:—ATROPIA and LINIM: BELLADON:

*BENZOINUM.
TINCT: BENZOIN: Co: contains gr. 44 to fl. ℥j.
Stimulant, Expectorant.
The Kidneys secrete it as Hippuric Acid.

BISMUTH: CARB: (D. gr. 5—20.)
Similar to Bismuth: Subnit:

BISMUTH: SUBNIT: (D. gr. 5—20.)
TROCH: BISMUTH: contain gr. 2 in each.
Sedative to Stomach and Intestines.
Pyrosis, Diarrhœa.
EXT: In Chronic Skin Diseases, and as a Cosmetic.

*BISMUTHUM.

---

† Messrs. ALLEN & HANBURY have prepared little squares of ATROPIA GELATINE, each containing rather more than gr. 1-1000 of Sulphate of Atropia, a very convenient and exact method of applying this powerful remedy to the Eye.

*BISMUTH: PURIF:

BORAX. (D. gr. 5—40.)
Sub-Astringent, Detergent, Diuretic, Emmenagogue.

*BROMUM.

*BUCHU FOL:

CADMII IODID:
Acts like Iodide of Lead, without the staining.
UNG: CADMII IOD: contains 1 part in 8.

CALCII CHLORID: (D. gr. 10—20.)
Alterative, Stimulant to the Lymphatics.
Allays Vomiting in certain cases.

CALC: CARB: PRÆCIP: (D. gr. 10—60.)
Similar to Creta Præp:

*CALC: HYDRAS.

CALC: PHOSPH: (D. gr. 10—20.)
Uncertain; used in Mollities Ossium.

CALUMBÆ RAD: (D. gr. 5—20.)
Bitter Stomachic and Tonic.
(May be given with Iron.)

*CALX.

CALX CHLORATA.
LIQ: CALC: CHLORAT: contains ℥ij to Oj.
Used as a disinfectant for Sick-rooms, &c.

CAMBOGIA. (D. gr. 1—4.)
PIL: CAMBOG: Co: contains 1 part in 6, nearly.
Drastic and Hydragogue Cathartic, Anthelmintic.
Obstinate Costiveness, Amenorrhœa, Dropsies.

CAMPHORA. (D. gr. 1—10.)
Stimulant and then Sedative, Calmative, Antispasmodic,
Diaphoretic.

*CANELLÆ ALB: CORT:
Aromatic, Stimulant.
Preparation:—VIN RHEI.

*CANNAB: IND:
Vide Ext: and Tinct: Cannab: Ind:

*CANTHARIS.
Vide Acetum Cantharid:, Chart: Epispas:, Emplas: Calefac:,
Emplas: Cantharid:, Liq: Epispas:, Tinct: Cantharid:
and Ung: Cantharid:

CAPSICI FRUCT: (D. gr. ½—1.)
    TINCT: CAPSICI, contains gr. 16½ to fl. ʒj.
        Acrid Stimulant.
           Scarlatina Maligna, Relaxed Sore Throat.

*CARBO ANIMAL:
CARBO ANIMAL: PURIF: (D. gr. 20—60.)
    Deodorizer for Sick-rooms.
        Diarrhœa, Dysentery, Dyspepsia.

CARBO LIGNI. (D. gr. 20—60.)
    Antiseptic, Disinfectant.

*CARDAMOMÙM.
    Aromatic.

*CARUI FRUCT:
    Stimulant, Carminative.

*CARYOPHYLLUM.
    Stimulant, Carminative.

*CASCARIL: CORT:
    Stimulant Tonic, Febrifuge.

*CASSIÆ PULP:
    CONFEC: SENNÆ contains 1 part in 8.
    Laxative; in large doses, Purgative.

CASTOREUM. (D. gr. 5—10.)
    Moderately Stimulant and Antispasmodic.
        Nervous and Spasmodic Affections.

CATAPLAS: CARBON:
    Applied to Foul Ulcers.

CATAPLAS: CONII.
    Soothing Application to Cancerous and other Sores.

CATAPLAS: FERMENTI.
    Stimulant and Antiseptic.

CATAPLAS: LINI.
    Emollient.

CATAPLAS: SINAP:
    Powerfully Rubefacient.
        Slight Inflammations, Head Affections, Spasms, Neuralgia.

CATAPLAS: SODÆ CHLOR:
    Disinfectant, Antiseptic, Stimulant.
        Foul Sores and Sloughing Ulcers.

CATECHU PALLID: (D. gr. 10—80.)
Powerful Astringent.
INF: CATECHU, contains gr. 16 to fl. ℥j.
PULV: CATECHU Co: contains 1 part in 2½.
TINCT: CATECHU, contains gr. 54½ to fl. ℥j.
TROCH: CATECHU, contains gr. 1 in each.
Diarrhœa, Atonic Dyspepsia, Hæmorrhages.

CERA ALBA.
Oleaginous Demulcent, Emollient.

CERA FLAVA.
Oleaginous Demulcent, Emollient.

CEREVIS: FERMENT: (D. ℥ss —j.)
EXT: Stimulant and Antiseptic.
INT: For prevention of Boils and Carbuncles, Diabetes. (?

CERII OXALAS. (D. gr. 1—2.)
Allays Vomiting, especially in Phthisis and Pregnancy.
Epilepsy, complicated with Stomach Derangement.

CETACEUM.
Oleaginous Demulcent, Emollient.

*CETRARIA.
DECOCT: CETRARIÆ, contains ℥j to Oj.

CHART: EPISPAS:
Vesicant.

*CHIRATA.
Vide Inf: and Tinct:

CHLOROFORMUM. (D. m. 3—10.)
LINIM: CHLOROFORM: contains 1 vol. in 2.
SPR: CHLOROFORM: contains 1 vol. in 20.
TINCT: CHLOROFORM: Co: contains 1 vol. in 10.
Narcotic, Antispasmodic, Stimulant and Cordial, Diphoretic.
When inhaled as an Anæsthetic, it produces:—
1st—Exhilaration.
2nd—Drowsiness (with excited manner).
3rd—Profound Sleep (Pupil contracted, and Breathing quiet.)
4th—Perfect Insensibility (stage for Surgical operations.
5th—Incipient Coma—Danger to Life (Pupil dilated).

CINCH: FLAV: CORT: (D. gr. 10—60.)
Vide Cinch: Rub:

CINCH: PALLID: CORT: (D. gr. 10—60.)
MIST: FER: AROMAT: ℥j to fl. ℥xvj.
> *Vide* Cinch: Rub:

CINCH: RUB: CORT: (D. gr. 10—60.)
Stomachic, Tonic, Astringent, Antiperiodic.
> *Vide* Quiniæ Sulph:

CINNAM: CORT:
Aromatic and Stomachic, Slightly Astringent.
> *Nausea, Flatulence, Cramps, Diarrhœa.*

*COCCUS.
For Colouring only.

COLCH: CORM: (D. gr. 2—8.)
Diuretic, Diaphoretic. Nauseant, Cathartic, Sedative and
Anodyne, Cholagogue, controls the Heart's action in
various Inflammatory complaints, augments Secretion of
Urea and Uric Acid.
> *Gout, Rheumatism, Dropsies.*

COLCH: SEM:
> *Vide* Colch: Corm:

COLLODIUM.
For protecting Inflamed and Tender Surfaces.

COLLODIUM FLEX:
Same use as Collodium.

COLOCYNTH: PULP: (D. gr. 2—8.)
EXT: COLOCYNTH: Co: contains 1 part in 4½, nearly.
PIL: COLOCYNTH: Co: contains 1 part in 6, nearly.
PIL: COLOCYNTH: ET HYOSCYAM, contains 1 part in 9, nearly.
Powerful Hydragogue Cathartic.

CONFECT: OPII. (D. gr. 5—20.)
Contains 1 part of Opium in 40, nearly,
> *Vide* Opium.

CONFECT: PIPER: (D. gr. 60—120.)
Gently Stimulant to the Alimentary Canal.

CONFECT: ROSÆ CANIN:
Acidulous, Astringent, Refrigerant.
> (℥j or more may be given—basis for Pills, &c.)

CONFECT: ROSÆ GALLIC:
Astringent.
> (℥j or more may be given—Vehicle or Pill basis.)

CONFECT: SCAM: (D. gr. 10—80.)
Stimulating Cathartic.

CONFECT: SENNÆ. (D. gr. 60—120.)
Mild Purgative.

CONFECT: SULPH: (D. gr. 60—120.)
Laxative Cathartic.

CONFECT: TEREBINTH: (D. gr. 60—120.)
Anthelmintic.

CONII FOLIA. (D. gr. 2—8.)
(Narcotic Poison,) Antispasmodic, Anodyne, Hypr
Deobstruent, Alterative.
Scirrhous, Cancer, Scrofula, Pertussis, Tetanus, Phth

CONII FRUCT:
Vide Conii Folia.

COPAIBA. (D. fl. ℥ss—j.)
Stimulant of Mucous surfaces, (especially Genito-urin
Cathartic, Diuretic.
Gonorrhœa, Gleet, &c.

*CORIAND: FRUCT:

CREASOTUM. (D. gtt. 1—8.)
MIST: CREASOT: m. 1 to fl. ℥j.
UNG: CREASOT: 1 part in 9.
INT: Stimulant, Antiseptic.
EXT: Chronic Skin disorders, Hœmorrhages, To
ache.
Vide Vapor Creasoti.

*CRETA.

CRETA PRÆP: (D. gr. 10—60.)
Antacid, Absorbent, Desiccant, indirectly Astringent.
In large and frequent doses apt to accumulate in
Intestines.

*CROCUS.
Slightly Stimulant.
(Chiefly used as a colouring agent.)

CUBEBA. (D. gr. 80—120.)
Stimulant, Stomachic.
Much used in Gonorrhœa.

CUPRI SULPHAS. { D. (gr. ½—2, Astringent.)
(gr. 5—10, Emetic.)
EXT: Caustic, Astringent.
INT: Astringent, Antispasmodic, Emetic.

*CUPRUM.

*CUSPARIÆ CORT:
Vide Infus: Cuspariæ.

CUSSO. (D. ℨij—iv.)
INFUS: CUSSO, ℨij in ℥iv.
Anthelmintic, (Tape-worm especially,) should be followed by a brisk purge.

OECOCT: ALOE: CO: (D. fl. ℥ſs—ij.)
Contains 4 grs. Aloe: Soc: to fl. ℥j.
Cathartic, Emmenagogue.

DECOCT: CETRARIÆ.
Demulcent, Tonic.
Phthisis, Chronic Pulmonary Complaints.

DECOCT: CINCH: FLAV: (D. fl. ℥j—ij.)
Stomachic, Tonic, Antiperiodic, Astringent.
(Better made with Acidulated Water.)

DECOCT: GRANATI RAD: (D. fl. ℥j—ij.)
Astringent, Anthelmintic.
Diarrhœa, Dysentery, Tape-worm.

DECOCT: HÆMATOX: (D. fl. ℥j—ij.)
Mild Astringent Tonic.
Diarrhœa, Hœmorrhagic Diathesis.

DECOCT: HORDEI. *(Ad lib.)*
Amylaceous and Mucilaginous Demulcent.

OECOCT: PAPAVER:
Emollient Anodyne Fomentation.
Painful and Inflamed Swellings, &c.

DECOCT: PAREIRÆ. (D. fl. ℥j—ij.)
Bitter Tonic, Diuretic.
Chronic Pyelitis, Irritable Bladder.

DECOCT: QUERCUS.
Used as a Lotion, Gargle, or Injection.
Relaxed Sore Throat, Leucorrhœa, Gonorrhœa, &c.
INT: fl. ℥j—ij may be given.

DECOCT: SARSÆ. (D. fl. ℨij—x.)
Alterative and Diaphoretic, Tonic, Diuretic.
Secondary Syphilis, Cachexia, Chronic Rheumatism.

DECOCT: SARSÆ CO: (D. fl. ℥ij—x.)
More Stimulating and Diaphoretic than the Simple D
tion.

DECOCT: SCOPARII. (D. fl. ℥ij–iv.)
Emetic and Cathartic, in large, Diuretic in small doses.
Dropsies depending on Heart Disease.

DECOCT: TARAXACI. (D. fl. ℥ij—iv.)
Aperient, Deobstruent, Alterative.
Liver and Cutaneous Affections.

DECOCT: ULMI. (D. fl. ℥ij—iv.)
Demulcent, Tonic.
Alterative in Skin Affections.

DIGITALINUM. (D. gr. $\frac{1}{60}$—$\frac{1}{30}$)
Indirectly Sedative, Diuretic.
*Heart Disease, Fevers, Inflammations, Dropsies, Pulmo
Affections, Nervous Irritability.*

DIGITALIS FOLIA. (D. gr. $\frac{1}{2}$—$1\frac{1}{2}$ in Powder.)
INFUS: DIGITALIS, gr. 8 to fl. ℥j.)
TINCT: DIGITALIS, gr. 54½ to fl. ℥j.)

*DULCAMARA.
Vide Infus: Dulcamaræ.

*ECBALII FRUCT:

ELATERIUM. (D. gr. $\frac{1}{16}$—$\frac{1}{4}$.)
Powerful Hydragogue Cathartic.
Hydrocephalus and other Dropsies.

*ELEMI.
Vide Ung: Elemi.

EMPLAST: AMMON: c: HYDRARG:
Stimulant to the Lymphatics.
*Glandular Enlargements, Chronic Inflammatory Proc
Nodes, &c.*

EMPLAST: BELLADON:
Anodyne. (Its efficiency is increased by sprinkling
plaster with Spt: Camph :)
Neuralgia.

EMPLAST: CALEFAC:
Stimulant to Tumours and Indolent Sores.

EMPLAST: CANTHARID:
Vesicant.

EMPLAST: CERAT: SAPON:
Emollient.
(But rather mechanically valuable.)

EMPLAST: FERRI.
Slightly Stimulant.
(Of questionable value beyond affording warmth and support.)

EMPLAST: GALBANI.
Stimulant and Discutient.

EMPLAST: HYDRARG:
Stimulant to the Lymphatics.
Enlargements of Joints and Glands, Chronic Tumours.

EMPLAST: OPII.
Contains 1 part in 10 of Opium.
For Rheumatic and other Pains.
Vide Opium.

EMPLAST: PICIS.
Calefacient and Rubefacient.

EMPLAST: PLUMBI.
Used for Strapping.

EMPLAST: PLUMBI IOD:
Mild Stimulant.
Enlarged Joints, Scrofulous Swellings.

EMPLAST: RESINÆ.
Used for Strapping, but more Stimulant than Emplast: Plumbi.

EMPLAST: SAPONIS.
Discutient.
Used for Strapping; only slightly irritant.

ENEMA ALOES.
40 grs. Aloe: Barb: vel Soc: in fl. ℥x.
Useful in Ascarides and Amenorrhœa.

ENEMA ASSAFŒT:
80 grs. in fl. ℥iv.
Antispasmodic, Stimulant.

ENEMA MAGN: SULPH:
℥j in fl. ℥xvj.
Purgative.

ENEMA OPII.
>Contains m. 15 of Tinct: in fl. ʒj.
>*Allays pain in Intestines, Bladder and Uterus.*

ENEMA TABACI.
>20 grs. to ʒviij of boiling water.
>*To produce Muscular Relaxation in cases of Strangul.*
>*Hernia.*

ENEMA TEREBINTH :
>fl. ʒj Ol: Terebinth: in fl. ʒxvj.
>Antispasmodic, Anthelmintic—(especially Ascarides

ERGOTA. (D. gr. 20—30.)
>Ext: Ergotæ Liquid : contains ʒj to fl. ʒj.
>Infus: Ergotæ, contains 11 grs. to fl. ʒj.
>Tinct: Ergotæ, contains 109 grs. to fl. ʒj.
>General Astringent, Emmenagogue.
>>*In Protracted Labour, from want of Uterine Powe*

ESS: ANISI. (D. m. 10—20.)
>Stimulant, Aromatic, Stomachic.
>*In Flatulent Colic.*

ESS: MENTH: PIP: (D. m. 10–20.)
>Stimulant, Carminative.
>*In Flatulency, Nausea, Griping.*

EXT: ACONITI. (D. gr. 1—2.)
>Anodyne and Diuretic.
>*Rheumatism, Gout, Neuralgia, Cancer, Heart Dise.*
>*Dropsies.*

EXT: ALOE: BARB: (D. gr. 2—6.)
>*Vide* Aloe: Soc:

EXT: ALOE: SOC: (D. gr. 2—6.)
>*Vide* Aloe: Soc:

EXT: ANTHEM: (D. gr. 2—10.)
>Aromatic Stomachic, Antiperiodic.
>*Atonic Dyspepsia.*

EXT: BELÆ LIQUID: (D. fl. ʒj—ij.)
>Astringent.
>*Diarrhœa, Dysentery.*

EXT: BELLADON: (D. gr. ¼—1.)
>Anodyne, Antispasmodic.
>>Ung: Belladon: contains gr. 80 to ʒj.
>>*Dilates Pupil when Topically applied. Incontin.*
>>*of Urine.*

EXT: CALUMBÆ. (D. gr. 2—10.)
Bitter Stomachic and Tonic.

EXT: CANNAB: IND: (D. gr. ¼—1.)
Antispasmodic and Anodyne, Soporific, Nervous Stimulant.
Hydrophobia, Asthma, Tetanus, Neuralgia. (Not followed by Constipation or Loss of Appetite.)

EXT: CINCH: FLAV: LIQUID: (D. m. 10—80.)
Stomachic, Tonic, Antiperiodic.

EXT: COLCH: (D. gr. ½—2.)
Vide Colch: Corm:

EXT: COLCH: ACET: (D. gr. ½—2.)
Vide Colch : Corm :
Especially suited for Gout, and as a Cholagogue.

EXT: COLOCYNTH: CO: (D. gr. 8—10.)
Contains 1 part Ext: Aloe: in 2½, nearly.
Powerful Hydragogue Cathartic.

EXT: CONII. (D. gr. 2—6.)
Pill : Conii Co: 2½ parts in 8.
Vide Conii Folia.

EXT: ERGOTÆ LIQUID: (D. m. 10—80.)
Each fl. ℨj contains ℨj of Ergot.
General Astringent, Emmenagogue.
In insufficient Uterine Contraction.

EXT: FILICIS LIQUID: (D. m. 15—30.)
Anthelmintic (especially Tapeworm,) should be followed by a Purgative.

EXT: GENTIANÆ. (D. gr. 2—10.)
Bitter Tonic, Antiperiodic, Anthelmintic.
Dyspepsia, Convalescences.

EXT: GLYCYR :
Employed as a Pill basis, and to cover the taste of nauseous Medicines.

EXT: HÆMATOX: (D. gr. 10—80.)
Astringent.

EXT: HYOSCYAMI. (D. gr. 5—10.)
Pill : Colocynth : et Hyoscyami, contains 1 part in 8.
Narcotic, Anodyne, Soporific.
Does not constipate the Bowels.

EXT: JALAPÆ. (D. gr. 5—15.)
Hydragogue Cathartic. (Less irritating than Scammony).

EXT: KRAMERIÆ. (D. gr. 5—20.)
Astringent, Tonic.

EXT: LACTUCÆ. (D. gr. 5—15.)
Anodyne, Diaphoretic, Slightly Diuretic.
Cough, Rheumatism, Nervous Irritability.

EXT: LUPULI. (D. gr. 5—15.)
Tonic, Stomachic, Narcotic.

EXT: MEZEREI ÆTH:
LINIM: SINAPIS Co: contains gr. 8 in fl. ℥j.
Epispastic.

EXT: NUCIS VOM: (D. gr. ½—2.)
Powerful Excitant of Spinal Cord, Bitter Stomachic, Stil
lant in cases of Paralysis, Tonic, and Antiperiodic. (?)

EXT: OPII. (D. gr. ½—2.)
About one part is obtained from two of Opium.
Preparations:—
EXT: OPII LIQUID: ℥j in Oj.
TROCH: OPII, gr. $\frac{1}{10}$ in each.
VIN: OPII, ℥j in Oj.
Vide Opium.

EXT: OPII LIQUID: (D. m. 10—40.)
22 grs. of Ext: in fl. ℥j, nearly.
Vide Opium.

EXT: PAPAVER: (D. gr. 2—5.)
Anodyne and Narcotic (without the nausea and irritat
effects of Opium).

EXT: PAREIRÆ. (D. gr. 10—20.)
Bitter Tonic, Diuretic.

EXT: PAREIRÆ LIQUID: (D. fl. ʒꟷij.)
Vide Decoct: Pareiræ.

+EXT: PHYSOSTIGMATIS. (D. gr. $\frac{1}{16}$—$\frac{1}{4}$.)
Topically it contracts the Pupil and diminishes Presbyop
INT: Sedative to Spinal Cord.

EXT: QUASSIÆ. (D. gr. 8—5.)
Bitter Tonic and Stomachic.

---

† Messrs. ALLEN & HANBURY have prepared little squares of GELAT
weighing gr. 1·50 each, and containing gr. 1·800 of Ext: Physostigmatis
convenient form for applying this potent remedy to the Eye.

EXT: RHEI. (D. gr. 5—15.)
Cathartic: in very small doses Stimulant and Tonic.

EXT: SARSÆ LIQUID: (D. fl. ℥ij—iv.)
Vide Decoct: Sarsæ.

EXT: STRAMONII. (D. gr. ¼—½.)
Anodyne, Antispasmodic.
    (Acts similar to Belladonna.)
       Neuralgia, Rheumatism, Mania.

EXT: TARAXACI. (D. gr. 5—80.)
Aperient, Deobstruent, Alterative.
    Some Liver Complaints and Chronic Skin Affections.

FARINA TRITICI.
Used in making Yeast Poultices.

FEL: BOV: PURIF: (D. gr. 5—10.)
Slightly Laxative and Stomachic.

FER: ARSENIAS. (D. gr. $\frac{1}{16}$—½.)
Tonic, Alterative.
    Agues, Neuralgia, Lepra, Chorea, &c.

FER: CARB: SACCH: (D. gr. 5—20.)
PIL: FER: CARB: contains 4 parts in 5.
    Anæmia. (This Preparation is not Astringent.)

FER: ET AMM: CITRAS. (D. gr. 5—10.)
Mild Ferruginous Tonic.
    (Not Astringent nor Irritant.)

FER: ET QUINÆ CITRAS: (D. gr. 5—10.)
A good combination of the two Tonics.

FER: IODID: (D. gr. 1—5.)
PIL: FER: IODID: contains 1 part in 8.
SYR: FER: IODID: contains 4·8 grs. in fl. ℥j.
    Chalybeate Tonic and Alterative.
      Anæmia, Scrofula, Constitutional Syphilis.

FER: OXID: MAGNET: (D. gr. 5—10.)
Chalybeate Tonic.
    Anæmia, Chlorosis, Amenorrhœa.

FER: PEROXID: HUMID: (D. ℥ij—iv.)
Ferruginous Tonic.
    Antidote in Poisoning by Arsenic.

FER: PEROXID: HYDRAT: (D. gr. 5–30.)
Ferruginous Tonic.
Tic-Doloreux.

FER: PHOSPHAS.   (D. gr. 5–10.)
SYR: FER: PHOSPH: gr. j in fl. ℨj.
Ferruginous Tonic.
Amenorrhœa, Caries, Mollities Ossium, Diabetes.

FER: SULPHAS.   (D. gr. 1–5.)
Irritant and Astringent Chalybeate.
Emmenagogue.

FER: SULPH: EXSIC: (D. gr. ½–8.)
Vide Fer: Sulph:

FER: SULPH: GRANULATA.   (D. gr. 1–5.)
Vide Fer: Sulph:

*FERRUM.

FER: REDACT: (D. gr. 1–5.)
Chalybeate Tonic.
Anœmia, Chlorosis, Amenorrhœa.

FER: TARTARAT: (D. gr. 5–10.)
Acts same as Fer: et Amm: Citras.
Compatible with Alkalis.

FICUS.
Saccharine Demulcent, slightly Laxative.

*FILIX MAS.
Vide Ext: Filicis Liquid:

*FŒNIC: FRUCT:
Vide Aq: Fœnic:

*GALBANUM.
PIL: ASSAFŒT: Co: 1 part in 8⅓.
Antispasmodic, Expectorant.

*GALLA.
Vide Acid: Gallic: and Acid: Tannic:

*GENTIAN: RAD:
Vide Ext: and Mist: Gentianæ and Infus: and Tinct: Gentianæ Co:

GLYCERINUM.   (D. fl. ℨj–ij.)
Sometimes used instead of Cod Liver Oil.   Readily dissolves Arsenious Acid, Borax, Vegetable Alkaloids and Acids. Soothing as an External Application.

GLYCER: ACID: CARBOL:
>One ounce Carbolic Acid to fl. ℥iv Glycerine.
>Antiseptic, Stimulant.

GLYCYR: ACID: GALLIC:
>One ounce Gallic Acid to fl. ℥iv Glycerine.
>Astringent.

GLYCER: ACID: TANNIC:
>One ounce Tannic Acid to fl. ℥iv Glycerine.
>Astringent.

GLYCER: AMYLI.
>One ounce Starch to fl. ℥viij Glycerine.
>Demulcent and Emollient.

GLYCER: BORACIS.
>One ounce Borax to fl. ℥iv Glycerine.
>Sub-Astringent.
>>*Aphthæ; applied to Throat and Tongue during Salivation.*

GLYCYR: RAD:
>Saccharine Demulcent.
>*Catarrhs, Urinary and Bowel Complaints.*

GOSSYPIUM.
>*Vide* Pyroxylin.

*GRANATI RAD: CORT:
>Astringent, Anthelmintic (gr. 20 powdered may be given).
>. *Vide* Decoct: Granati: Cort:

*GUAIACI LIGN:
GUAIACI RES: (D. gr. 10 - 30.)
>MIST: GUAIACI, 11 gr. in fl. ℥j.
>TINCT: GUAIACI AMMONIAT: 88 grs. in fl. ℥j.
>>Acrid Stimulant, Diaphoretic, Alterative, Irritant to Intestines, Purgative in large doses.
>>*Chronic Rheumatism, Constitutional Syphilis, Scrofula, Chronic Skin Affections, Dysmenorrhœa.*

*HÆMATOX: LIGN:
>Mild Astringent and Tonic in form of Decoct: and Ext:

*HEMIDESMI RAD:
>Used as a substitute for Sarsaparilla.
>>*Cutaneous Affections of Syphilis, various Kidney diseases.*

HIRUDO.
1.—The Speckled Leech (from the more northern parts Europe).
2.—The Green Leech (from the more southern parts Europe).

*HORDEUM DECORT :
Preparation:—DECOCT: HORDEI.

HYDRARG : IODID : RUB : (D. gr. $\frac{1}{16}$—$\frac{1}{4}$.)
UNGT : HYDRARG : IOD : RUB : contains 1 part in 28.
Alterative. (Acts similar to Corrosive Sublimate.)
Scrofula, Skin Affections.

HYDRARG : IODID : VIR : (D. gr. 1—8.)
Alterative Stimulant. (Acts similar to Calomel.)
Syphilis, Scrofula.

*HYDRARG : OXID : RUB :
UNGT : HYDRARG : OXID : RUB : contains 1 part in 8.
Irritant Stimulant.

HYDRARG : PERCHLOR : (D. gr. $\frac{1}{16}$—$\frac{1}{8}$.)
(HYDRARG : CORROSIV : SUBLIM :, 1864.)
LIQUOR : HYDRARG : PERCHLOR : gr. $\frac{1}{2}$ in fl. 3j.
LOT : HYDRARG : FLAV : contains gr. 18 to fl. 3x.
Caustic, Alterative, Sialogogue.
Syphilis, Chronic Cutaneous Affections.

HYDRARG : SUBCHLOR : (D. gr. $\frac{1}{2}$—5.)
(CALOMEL, 1864.)
PIL : HYDRARG : SUBCHLOR : Co : 1 part in 5.
LOT : HYDRARG : NIG : contains gr. 8 to fl. 3j.
UNGT : HYDRARG : SUBCHLOR : contains 1 pt. in 6$\frac{1}{2}$, nea
Alterative, Stimulant, Cathartic, Antiphlogistic.
Syphilis, Liver Affections, Skin Diseases.

*HYDRARG : SULPHAS.

*HYDRARGYRUM.

*HYDRARG : AMMONIAT :
UNGT : HYDRARG : AMMONIAT : contains 1 part in 8.

HYDRARG : C : CRETÂ. (D. gr. 8—8.)
Contains 1 part Mercury in 8 parts.
Alterative, Cathartic, Antacid.

HYOSCYAMI FOLIA.
Vide Ext : Hyoscyami.

INFUS: ANTHEM: (D. fl. ʒj—iv.)
Aromatic Stomachic and Tonic; Emetic in large doses.

INFUS: AURANT: (D. fl. ʒj—ij.)
Slightly Stomachic and Tonic.

INFUS: AURANT: CO: (D. fl. ʒj—ij.)
Warm Tonic Stomachic.

INFUS: BUCHU. (D. fl. ʒj—iv.)
Tonic, Diuretic.
Some Affections of Urinary Organs.

INFUS: CALUMBÆ. (D. fl. ʒj—ij.)
Bitter Stomachic and Tonic.

INFUS: CARYOPH: (D. fl. ʒj—iv.)
Warm Carminative; as a Vehicle.

INFUS: CASCARIL: (D. fl. ʒj—ij.)
Light Warm Tonic.

INFUS: CATECHU. (D. fl. ʒj—ij.)
Powerful Astringent.

INFUS: CHIRATÆ. (D. fl. ʒj—ij.)
Bitter Tonic in Convalescence, Stomachic in Dyspepsia.

INFUS: CINCH: FLAV: (D. fl. ʒj—ij.)
Stomachic, Tonic, Antiperiodic; Ext: Antiseptic.
(Better made with Acidulated Water.)

INFUS: CUSPARIÆ. (D. fl. ʒj—ij.)
Stimulant Tonic, Febrifuge, Antidysenteric.

INFUS: CUSSO. (D. fl. ʒiv.—viij.)
Anthelmintic. (Should be followed by a Purge.)

INFUS: DIGITALIS. (D. fl. ʒij—iv.)
Vide Digitalinum.

INFUS: DULCAMARÆ. (D. fl. ʒj—ij.)
Alterative, slightly Narcotic.
Acts gently on Skin and Kidneys.
Cutaneous Affections.

INFUS: ERGOTÆ. (D. fl. ʒj—ij.)
Vide Ergota.

INFUS: GENTIAN: CO: (D. fl. ʒj—ij.)
Aromatic Tonic and Stomachic.
Useful to combine with Acids.

INFUS: KRAMERIÆ. (D. fl. ℥j—ij.)
Astringent, Tonic.

INFUS: LINI.
Fomentations, Enemata.

INFUS: LUPULI. (D. fl. ℥j—ij.)
Tonic, Slightly Narcotic.

INFUS: MATICÆ. (D. fl. ℥j—iv.)
Supposed to act as an Astringent on the Urinary Organs.

INFUS: QUASSIÆ. (D. fl. ℥j—ij.)
Bitter Tonic and Stomachic.

INFUS: RHEI. (D. fl. ℥j—ij.)
Aperient and Stomachic.

INFUS: ROSÆ ACID. (D. fl. ℥j—ij.)
Slightly Astringent and Tonic.
Contains m. 10 ACID: SULPH: DIL: to fl. ℥j.

INFUS: SENEGÆ. (D. ℥j—ij.)
Stimulant, Sialogogue, Expectorant, Diaphoretic, Diuretic,
Emmenagogue.

INFUS: SENNÆ. (D. fl. ℥j—ij.)
Warm Purgative.

INFUS: SERPENTAR: (D. fl. ℥j—ij.)
Diaphoretic, Stimulant, Tonic, Emmenagogue.

INFUS: UVÆ URSI: (D. fl. ℥j—ij.)
Astringent, Tonic, Mild Diuretic.
Genito-Urinal Affections, Diseases of the Kidneys.

INFUS: VALERIAN: (D. fl. ℥j—ij.)
Moderately Stimulant and Antispasmodic.

*****IODUM.**

IPECACUANHA. { D. (Expectorant, gr. ¼—2.)
(Emetic, gr. 15—30.)
PIL: CONII CO: contains 1 part in 6.
PIL: IPECAC: c: SCILLÁ, 1 part in 16½, nearly.
PULV: IPECAC: CO: 1 part in 10.
TROCH: IPECAC: gr. ¼ in each.
TROCH: MORPHIÆ ET IPECAC: gr. $\frac{1}{12}$ in each.
VIN: IPECAC: 22 grs. to fl. ℥j.
Expectorant, Diaphoretic, Laxative, Alterative, Nauseant,
Emetic.
*Catarrh, Diarrhœa, Ague; as an Emetic in Bronchitis,
Phthisis, Croup.*

JALAPA. (D. gr. 10—80.)
  PULV: JALAPÆ Co: contains 1 part in 8.
  PULV: SCAM: Co: contains 8 parts in 8.
  TINCT: JALAPÆ, contains 54½ grs. to fl. ℥j.
    Hydragogue, Cathartic. (Less irritating than Scammony.)

JALAPÆ RES: (D. gr. 2—5.)
  Hydragogue, Cathartic.
    A good Anthelmintic when joined with Hydrarg: Sub-
    chlor.

KAMALA. (D. gr. 80—ʒij.)
  Purgative and Powerful Anthelmintic (especially Tape-worm).

KINO. (D. gr. 10—80.)
  PULV: CATECHU Co: 1 part in 5.
  PULV: KINO Co: 8¾ parts in 5.
  TINCT: KINO ℥ij to Oj.
    Powerful Astringent.
      Pyrosis, Diarrhœa, Relaxed Throat.

*KRAMER: RAD:
  Preparations:—EXT:, INFUS:, and TINCT: KRAMERIÆ.
    PULV: CATECHU Co: contains 1 part in 5.

LAC.
  Used in Mist: Scam:

*LACTUCA.
  Vide Ext: Lactucæ.

*LAUROCERASI FOLIA.
  Vide Aq: Laurocerasi.

*LIMON: CORT:
  Aromatic and Tonic Stomachic.

*LIMON: SUC:
  SYR: LIMON: contains Oj to 8½ pounds.
    Refrigerant, Antalkaline, Antiscorbutic.
      Rheumatism. (D. fl. ℥j—iv.)

LINI FARINA.
  An Emollient basis for Cataplasms.

*LINI SEM:

LINIM: ACONITI.
  Neuralgia, Chronic Rheumatic Pains.

LINIM: AMMONIÆ.
  Stimulant and Rubefacient.

LINIM : BELLADON :

Anodyne.

Dilates Pupil when used locally. Neuralgia, Cardalgi Spasmodic contraction of the Urethra.

LINIM : CALCIS.

Excellent application for Burns and Scalds.

LINIM : CAMPH :

LINIM : CHLOROFORMI, contains 1 vol. in 2.
LINIM : TEREBINTH : ACET : contains 1 vol. in 8.
Stimulant and Anodyne.

LINIM : CAMPH : CO :

Rubefacient and Stimulant.

LINIM : CHLOROFORMI.

Anodyne, Stimulant.

Allays Itching in some Skin Diseases.

LINIM : CROTONIS.

Strongly Counter-Irritant, causing Pustulation.

LINIM : HYDRARG :

Stimulant to the Absorbents.

Indolent Tumours and Swellings.

LINIM : IODI.

Alterative and Absorbent.

Chronic Skin Diseases, Chronic Indurations.

LINIM : OPII.

1 vol : of TINCT : in 2 vols :

Allays Pain, and produces general effects of Opium.

LINIM : POTAS : IOD : c : SAPONE.

Mild Alterative and Absorbent.

LINIM : SAPONIS.

Emollient and Stimulant.

LINIM : SINAP : CO :

Strongly Rubefacient.

LINIM : TEREBINTH :

Stimulant. Sometimes applied to Burns and Scalds.

Chronic Inflammation, and Pain of various sorts.

LINIM : TEREBINTH : ACET :

More effective than Linim : Terebinth :

*LIQ: AMMONIÆ.
Used for making Linim: Ammoniæ. (1 vol. in 4.)
Antacid, Antispasmodic, Stimulating Expectorant; in
large doses, Emetic; in larger, Poisonous.

LIQ: AMMON: ACET: (D. fl. ℥ij—vj.)
Diaphoretic, Refrigerant, Diuretic.
Dysmenorrhœa.

LIQ: AMMON: CITRAT: (D. fl. ℥ij—vj.)
Diaphoretic, Refrigerant.

*LIQ: AMMON: FORT:

*LIQ: ANTIMON: CHLOR:

LIQ: ARSENICALIS. (D. m. 2—8.)
Contains 4 grs. ACID: ARSENIOSUM in fl. ℥j.
Antiperiodic, Alterative.
Agues, Neuralgia, &c.

LIQ: ARSENICI HYDROCHLOR: (D. m. 2—8.)
Contains 4 grs. ARSENICI HYDROCHLOR: in fl. ℥j.
Agues, Neuralgia, Skin Diseases, Chorea, Gastrodynia.
(Less irritating to the Stomach than Liq: Arsenicalis.)

*LIQ: ATROPIÆ.
Contains gr. 4 in fl. ℥j.
Vide Atropiæ Sulph:

LIQ: ATROPIÆ SULPH:
Contains gr. 4 in fl. ℥j.
Vide Atropiæ Sulph:

LIQ: BISMUTH: ET AMMON: CITRAT: (D. fl. ℥ſs—j.)
Sedative and Refrigerant to the Stomach, Diaphoretic.

LIQ: CALCIS. (D. fl. ℥j—iv.)
Antacid, Astringent.
Dyspepsia, Diarrhœa, Lithic Diathesis.

*LIQ: CALCIS CHLOR:
Disinfectant and Antiseptic.

LIQ: CALCIS SACCH: (D. m. 15—60.)
Antacid, Astringent.
Dyspepsia, Diarrhœa.

LIQ: CHLORI. (D. m. 10—20.)
Disinfectant, Antiseptic, Stimulant.
Typhoid, Scarlatina Maligna.

LIQ: EPISPAS:
Ext: Rubefacient, Vesicant.

LIQ: FER: PERCHLOR: (D. m. 10—80.)
Very powerful Astringent, Tonic, Diuretic.
Passive Hæmorrhages, Anæmia.

LIQ: FER: PERCHLOR: FORT:
Liq: Fer: Perchlor: contains 1 vol. in 4.
Tinct: Fer: Perchlor: contains 1 vol. in 4.
Ext: in Hœmorrhages.

LIQ: FER: PERNITRAT: (D. m. 10—40.)
Acts similarly to Liq: Fer: Perchlor:
Diarrhœa with Debility, Passive Mucous Discharges.

*LIQ: FER: PERSULPH:

LIQ: HYDRARG: NITRAT: ACID:
Powerful Caustic.
Cancerous Affections, Lupus, Skin Affections.

LIQ: HYDRARG: PERCHLOR: (D. fl. 3ß—ij.)
Gr. ½ in fl. ℥j.
Alterative, Sialogogue.
Syphilis, Chronic Skin Affections, Nodes, &c.

LIQ: IODI.
Counter-Irritant, Vesicant.

LIQ: LITHIÆ EFFERVES: (D. fl. ℥v—x.)
(Lithia Water.)
Diuretic.
Forms a soluble compound with Uric Acid.
Gout, Uric Acid Deposits.

LIQ: MAGNES: CARB: (D. fl. ℥j—ij.)
18 grs. to fl. ℥j.
Laxative, Watery Purge, Diuretic.

LIQ: MORPHIÆ ACET: (D. m. 10—60.)
4 grs. of Acetate in fl. ℥j.
Vide Morphiæ Acet:

LIQ: MORPHIÆ HYDROCHLOR: (D. m. 10 - 60.)
4 grs. of Hydrochlorate in fl. ℥j.
Not so liable to decompose as the Solution of the Aceta
Vide Morphiæ Hydrochlor.

*LIQ: PLUMB: SUBACET ·

LIQ: PLUMB: SUBACET: DIL:
Contains Liq : Plumb : Subacet : fl. ℥ij in Oj.
Soothing and Astringent.
Skin Affections, Inflamed Parts.

LIQ: POTASSÆ. (D. m. 15—60.)
Antacid, Alterative, Sedative.
Serous Inflammations, Syphilis, Rheumatism, Scrofula.

LIQ: POTAS: EFFERVES:
(Potash Water.)
Antacid, Antilithic, Diuretic.

LIQ: POTAS: PERMANGAN: (D. fl. ℨij—iv.)
Strong Antiseptic.
Diabetes. As a Gargle in Sore Throat, &c.

*LIQ: SODÆ.
Used in preparing other Compounds.

LIQ: SODÆ ARSENIATIS. (D. m. 5—10.)
Vide Liq : Arsenicalis and Liq : Arsenici Hydrochlor:

LIQ: SODÆ CHLORATÆ. (D. m. 10—20.)
Disinfectant, Antiseptic, Stimulant.
Low Malignant Fevers.

LIQ: SODÆ EFFERVES:
(Soda Water.)
Stomachic Stimulant, followed by Alkaline reaction.

LIQ: STRYCHNIÆ. (D. m. 5—10.)
Vide Strychnia.

LIQ: ZINCI CHLOR.
Vide Zinci Chlor :
Antiseptic, Caustic, Disinfectant.

LITHIÆ CARB: (D. gr. 3—6.)
Diuretic.
Gout, Uric Acid Deposits.

LITHIÆ CITRAS. (D. gr. 5—10.)
Similar to Lithiæ Carb :

*LOBELIA.
Preparations :—
TINCT: LOBELIA
TINCT: LOBELIA ÆTH : } Contain 54¼ grs. to fl. ℥j.

LOTIO HYDRARG: FLAV:
> HYDRARG : PERCHLOR:, gr. 18 to Oʒ.
> *Chronic Skin Affections, Chronic Discharges from Mu*
> *Surfaces.*

LOTIO HYDRARG: NIG:
> HYDRARG: SUBCHLOR:, gr. 30 to Oʒ.
> Stimulant.
>> *Chronic Varicose and other Sores, Gonorrhœa.*

*LUPULUS.
> *Vide* Ext:, Infus:, and Tinct: Lupuli.
> (Hypnotic in the form of a Pillow.)

MAGNESIA. (D. gr. 10—60.)
> PULV : RHEI Co : contains 6 parts in 9.
> *Vide* Magnes: Levis.

MAGNES: LEVIS. (D. gr. 10—60.)
> Antacid, Laxative, Purgative.
>> *Acid Dyspepsia, Gout, Diarrhœa, Urinary Deposits*
>> *Acidity.*
>>> (Apt to concrete in the Bowels if given for too lo
>>> time.)

MAGNES: CARB: (D. gr. 10—60.)
> LIQ : MAGNES : CARB: contains gr. 18 in fl. ʒj.
> TROCH : BISMUTH :, gr. 2½ in each.
> Similar to Magnes ; Levis.

MAGNES: CARB: LEVIS. (D. gr. 10—60.)
> Similar to Magnes: Levis.

MAGNES: SULPH : (D. gr. 60—ʒʒ.)
> Preparations:—
> ENEMA MAGNES: SULPH : ʒj to fl. ʒxvj.
> MIST : SENNÆ Co : ʒj to fl. ʒv.
> Cathartic, Diuretic.
>> *Febrile Affections, Portal Congestion,*

*MANGANESII OXID: NIG:
> Used for producing Chlorine.

MANNA. (D. gr. 60—ʒj.)
> Mild Laxative.

*MARMOR: ALB:
> Used for producing Carbonic Acid Gas.

°MASTICHE.
Similar to Turpentine resin. May be given in doses of gr. 20—40.

MATICÆ FOL:
Mechanically Hœmostatic.
(Contains only a trace of Tannic or Gallic Acid.)

MEL.
Saccharine Demulcent.
Used as a Vehicle and Adjunct.

MEL BORACIS.
Apthæ; applied to Throat and Tongue during Salivation.

MEL DEPUR:
MEL BORACIS, 8 parts in 9, nearly.
CONFECT: PIPER, 15 parts in 20.
CONFECT: SCAM:, 1½ part in 10.
CONFECT: TEREBINTH:, 1 part in 2, nearly.
OXYMEL, 40 parts in 50.

MEZEREI CORT:
Vide Ext: Mezerei Æth:
Moistened with Vinegar it Blisters the Skin upon a second or third application.

MICA PANIS.
Used for Emollient Cataplasms, and for giving consistence to Pills.

MIST: AMMONIACI. (D. fl. ʒꝶ—j.
Antispasmodic, Expectorant.
Chronic Bronchitis.
EXT: Stimulant Discutient.

MIST: AMYGD: (D. fl. ʒj—ij.)
Demulcent.
Principally used as a Vehicle.

MIST: CREASOTI. (D. fl. ʒj—ij.)
Stimulant, Antiseptic.
Diabetes. Some forms of Vomiting.

MIST: CRETÆ. (D. fl. ʒj—ij.)
Antacid, Astringent, Demulcent.
Diarrhœa.

MIST: FERRI AROMAT: (D. fl. ʒj—ij.)
Tonic, Antiperiodic.
Debility with Anæmia.

MIST: FERRI CO: (D. fl. ℥j—ij.)
Tonic, Emmenagogue.
Anæmic Amenorrhœa.

MIST: GENTIAN: (D. fl. ℥ß—j.)
Aromatic Tonic and Stomachic.
Dyspepsia and Convalescences.

MIST: GUAIACI. (D. fl. ℥ß—ij.)
Vide Guaiaci Res:
11 grs. in each fl. ℥j.

MIST: SCAM: (D. fl. ℥ß—ij, for a Child.)
Contains 2 grs. Scam: to fl. ℥j.
Cathartic.

MIST: SENNÆ CO: (D. fl. ℥j—iß.)
Stimulating Saline Purgative.

MIST: SPT: VINI GALLICI. (D. fl. ℥j—ij.)
Diffusible Stimulant.
*Typhus, Syncope, Senile Gangrene, and other low state
the system.*

MORI SUC:
Refrigerant. (Also a Colouring Agent.)

MORPHIÆ ACET: (D. gr. ⅛—½.)
(1 part is obtained from 8 or 10 parts of Opium.)
Preparation:—LIQ: MORPHIÆ ACET: contains gr. 1 in fl. ℥i
Less stimulating than Opium. Often used endermically
allay pain.

MORPHIÆ HYDROCHLOR: (D. gr. ⅛—½.)
(1 part is obtained from 8 or 10 parts of Opium.)
Preparations:—
LIQ: MORPHIÆ HYDROCHLOR:, gr. 1 in fl. ℥ij.
SUPPOS: MORPHIÆ, gr. ½ in each.
TROCH: MORPHIÆ, gr. $\frac{1}{36}$ in each.
TROCH: MORPHIÆ ET IPECAC:, gr. $\frac{1}{36}$ in each.
Same uses as Morphiæ Acet:

MOSCHUS. (D. gr. 5—10.)
Stimulant, Antispasmodic, Hypnotic, Aphrodisiac (?).
Nervous Affections.

MUCILAG: ACACIÆ.
Demulcent.
Useful for suspending heavy Powders.

MUCILAG: AMYLI.
Demulcent.
As an Injection in Dysentery and Urinary Affections.
As a vehicle for heavy Powders.

MUCILAG: TRAGACANTH:
Demulcent.
Used for making Pills, and as a vehicle for heavy
Powders.

***MYRISTICA.**
An Aromatic and Stimulating adjunct to several Preparations.

***MYRRHA.**
Preparations:—
DECOCT: ALOE: Co:, gr. 8 to fl. 3j.
MIST: FER: Co:, gr. 6 to fl. 3j.
PIL: ALOE: ET MYRRH:, 1 part in 6.
PIL: ASSAFŒT: Co:, 1 part in 8½.
PIL: RHEI Co:, 1 part in 8, nearly.
TINCT: MYRRH:, gr. 54½ to fl. 3j.
Stomachic Tonic, Expectorant, Antispasmodic, Emmena-
gogue. Dose, gr. 10—80.

***NECTANDRÆ CORT:**
Vide Beberiæ Sulphas.

***NUX VOMICA.**
TINCT: NUCIS VOMICÆ, contains 44 grs. to fl. 3j.
Vide Ext: Nucis Vomicæ, and Strychnia.

OL: AMYGD:
Oleaginous Demulcent, Emollient.
Used in several Ointments. Dose, fl. 3j—iv.

OL: ANETHI.
Vide Aq: Anethi.
Dose, m. 1—5.

OL: ANISI.
Preparations:—
ESS: ANISI, 1 vol. in 5.
TINCT: CAMPH: Co:, fl. 3ß to Oj.
TINCT: OPII AMMONIAT:, fl. 3j to Oj.
Dose, m. 1—5.

OL: ANTHEMID:
Stimulant and Carminative.
Dose, m. 1—5.

c 8

OL: CAJUPUTI.

Preparations:
LINIM: CROTONIS, 8½ vols. in 8.
SPT: CAJUPUTI, 1 vol. in 50.

Strongly Stimulant and Antispasmodic.
Colic, Hysteria, Cholera, Chronic Rheumatism.
EXT: *Gouty and Rheumatic Parts.*
Dose, m. 1—5.

OL: CARUI.

Vide Aq: Carui:
Dose, m. 1—5.

OL: CARYOPH:

Stimulant, Aromatic, Carminative.
Atonic Dyspepsia, Tooth-ache. Dose, m. 1—5.

OL: CINNAM:

Powerful Stimulant.
Dose, m. 1—5.

OL: COPAIBÆ. (D. m. 5—29.)

Cathartic, Diuretic, Stimulant of Mucous Surfaces (especially of Urinary Organs).
Gonorrhea, Gleet, Chronic Bronchitis, Diseases of Mucous Membrane of Rectum.

OL: CORIAND:

Stimulant, Aromatic, Carminative.
Dose, m. 1—5.

OL: CROTON: (D. m. ½—1.)

INT: Drastic Purgative.
EXT: Counter-Irritant, Vesicant.

OL: CUBEB: (D. gtt. 5—20.)

Stimulant, Stomachic.
Arrests discharge in Gonorrhœa.

OL: JUNIPER:

Vide Spt: Juniper:
Dose, m. 1—10.

OL: LAVAND:

Stimulant, Carminative.
Hysteria, Hypochondriasis, Colic. Dose, m. 1—5.

OL: LIMON:

Contained in Linim: Potas: Iod: c. Sapone and Spt:
Ammon: Aromat:

Dose, m. 1—5.

OL: LINI.

Emollient, Cathartic.

OL: MENTH: PIP:

Preparations:—

Aq: Menth: Pip:, fl. 3iß to Cj.
Ess: Menth: Pip:, 1 vol. in 5.
Pil: Rhei Co:, m. 1 in 3j, nearly.
Spt: Menth: Pip:, 1 vol. in 50.

Stimulant, Carminative.

Dose, m. 1—5.

OL: MENTH: VIR:

Stimulant, Carminative.

Dose, m. 1—5.

OL: MORRHUÆ. (D. fl. 3j—viij.)

An easily-assimilated Oil. Nourishing and valuable in
· *Phthisis, Scrofula, Cachexia; various Skin Affections;
Chronic Rheumatism and Gout; Neuralgia.*

OL: MYRIST:

Aromatic, Stimulant.

Dose, m. 1—5.

Vide Spt: Myrist:

OL: MYRIST: EXPRES:

Emollient and Stimulant.

Enters into Emplas: Calefac: and Emplas: Picis.

OL: OLIVÆ.

Oleaginous Demulcent, Emollient.

Used in many Preparations.

Dose, fl. 3j—viij.

OL: PIMENTÆ.

Stimulant, Aromatic, Carminative.

Atonic Dyspepsia, Flatulence.

Dose, m. 1—5.

OL: RICINI. (D. fl. 3j—viij.)

Gentle Purgative (acting without irritation).

Gastritis, Dysentery.

OL: ROSMAR:
> LINIM: SAPON:, fl. 3j to fl. ʒvij, nearly.
> SPT: ROSMAR:, 1 vol. in 50.
> TINCT: LAVAND: Co:, m. 5 to Oj.
>> Powerful Stimulant, Carminative.
>> *Hysteria, Nervous Head-aches.*
>>> Dose, m. 1—5.
>> EXT: Rubefacient.

OL: RUTÆ.
> Powerful Stimulant, Antispasmodic, Emmenagogue, Anthel-
> mintic.
>> *Epilepsy, Hysteria.*
>> Dose, m. 1—5.

OL: SABINÆ. (D. m. 1—5.)
> Irritant, Strongly Emmenagogue.
>> Dose, m. 1—5.
>> EXT: As an Irritant after Blisters and Setons.

OL: SINAPIS.
> LINIM: SINAPIS Co: contains 1 vol. in 41.
>> Stimulant and Vesicant.

OL: TEREBINTH: (D. m. 10 to fl. ʒꭥ.)
> CONFECT: TEREBINTH:, 1 part in 4, nearly.
> ENEMA: TEREBINTH:, 1 vol. in 16.
> LINIM: TEREBINTH:, 16 parts in 19, nearly.
> LINIM: TEREBINTH: ACET:, 1 vol. in 8.
> UNG: TEREBINTH:, 1 part in 2, nearly.
>> EXT: Rubefacient, Counter-Irritant.
>> INT: Stimulant, Diuretic, Diaphoretic, Cathartic, Anthel-
>> mintic, Antispasmodic, Astringent.

OL: THEOBROMÆ.
> Emollient. (Much used as a Vehicle.)

OPIUM. (D. gr. ½—2.)
> Preparations containing Opium:—
> CONFECT: OPII, 1 part in 40, nearly.
> EMPLAST: OPII, 1 part in 10.
> ENEMA OPII, fl. ʒꭥ TINCT: to fl. ʒij.
> EXT: OPII, about 1 part from 2.
> EXT: OPII LIQUID:, 22 grs. EXT: in fl. ʒj, nearly.
> LINIM: OPII, 1 vol. TINCT: in 2 vols.
> MORPHIÆ ACET:, about 1 part from 8 or 10.
> MORPHIÆ ACET: LIQ:, 4 grs. ACET: in fl. ʒj.
> MORPHIÆ HYDROCHLOR:, about 1 part from 8 or 10.

MORPHIÆ HYDROCHLOR : LIQ :, 4 grs. HYDROCHLOR : in fl. ℥j.
PIL : IPECAC : c. SCILLA, 1 part in 16½, nearly.
PIL : PLUMB : c. OPIO, 1 part in 8.
PIL : SAPONIS Co:, 1 part in 6, nearly.
PULV : CRETÆ AROMAT : c. OPIO, 1 part in 40.
PULV : IPECAC : Co :, 1 part in 10.
PULV : KINO Co:, 1 part in 20.
PULV : OPII Co :, 1 part in 10.
SUPPOS : PLUMB : Co:, 1 gr. in each suppository.
TINCT : CAMPH : Co :, 2 grs. to fl. ℥j.
TINCT : OPII, 83 grs. to fl. ℥j, nearly.
TINCT : OPII AMMONIAT :, 5 grs. to fl. ℥j.
TROCH : OPII, $\frac{1}{10}$ gr. in each.
UNG : GALLÆ c. OPIO, 32 grs. to ℥j.
VIN : OPII, 22 grs. EXT : to fl. ℥j, nearly.

> Opium first excites the vascular and nervous systems,
> exalting the mental functions, producing pleasant sen-
> sations, followed by drowsiness and sound sleep, and
> frequently with perspiration. On awaking there is
> nausea, loss of appetite, thirst, torpor of bowels. The
> stimulating effect continues on an average for half-an-
> hour.

Uses :—EXT : Stimulant, then Sedative.
> INT : Sedative, Anodyne, Hypnotic, Diaphoretic, Anti-
> spasmodic, Febrifuge.

*OS USTUM.
Used in preparing Calc : Phosph : and Sodæ Phosph :

OVI VITELLUS.
Preparation :—MIST : SPT : VIN : GALLIC :
> Dietetic and Nutrient. Albuminous Demulcent.

OXYMEL. (D. fl. ℥j—ij.)
Slightly Expectorant and Diaphoretic.

OXYMEL SCILLÆ. (D. fl. ℈ss—j.)
Expectorant and Diaphoretic.
> Sometimes used as an Emetic for Children.

PAPAVER : CAPSULÆ.
Vide Decoct : Syr : and Ext : Papaver :

*PAREIRÆ RAD :
Vide Decoct : and Ext : Pareiræ.
> Bitter Tonic, Diuretic.
>> (May be given in Powder. D. gr. 20—80.)

PHOSPHORUS.
Vide Acid : Phosph : Dil :

PHYSOSTIGMATIS FABA. (D. gr. 1—4, in Powder.)
Vide Ext: Physostigmatis.

PIL: ALOE: BARB: (D. gr. 5—10.)
1 part Aloes in 2, nearly.
Cathartic and Tonic.

PIL: ALOE: ET ASSAFŒT: (D. gr. 5—10.)
1 part Aloes and 1 part Assafœt: in 4.
Purgative and Antispasmodic.
Chronic Dyspepsia, &c.

PIL: ALOE: ET FER: (D. gr. 5—10.)
1 part Aloes in 5¼, and 1 part Fer: Sulph: in 7.
Chalybeate Laxative and Tonic.
Amenorrhœa, Anœmia.

PIL: ALOE: ET MYRRH: (D. gr. 5—10.)
1 part Aloes in 8.
Amenorrhœa, Anœmia.

PIL: ALOE: SOC: (D. gr. 5—10.)
1 part Aloes in 2, nearly.
Cathartic and Tonic.

PIL: ASSAFŒT: CO: (D. gr. 5—10.)
1 part Assafœt: and 1 part Galbanum in 8¼.
Antispasmodic, Stimulant, Expectorant.
Hysteria, &c.

PIL: CAMBOG: CO: (D. grs. 5—10.)
1 part Cambog: and 1 part Aloes in 6, nearly.
Hydragogue Purge, Anthelmintic.
Amenorrhœa, Dropsies.

PIL: COLOCYNTH: CO: (D. gr. 5—10.)
1 part Aloes and 1 part Scammonium in 8, and 1 part
Colocynth: Pulp: in 6, nearly.
Powerful Hydragogue Cathartic.
(Less griping and irritating than Colocynth: Pulp:)

PIL: COLOCYNTH: ET HYOSCYAMI. (D. gr. 5—10.)
2 parts Pil: Colocynth: Co: and 1 part Ext: Hyoscyam:
Hydragogue Cathartic.
(Less griping and irritating than Pil: Colocynth: Co:)

PIL: CONII CO: (D. gr. 5—10.)
5 parts Ext: Conii and 1 part Ipecacuanha in 6.
Anodyne Expectorant.
Spasmodic Cough.

PIL: FER: CARB: (D. gr. 5—20.)
> 4 parts Fer: Carb: Sacch: in 5.
>> Ferruginous Tonic. (Not Astringent.)
>>> *Anæmic Amenorrhœa.*

PIL: FER: IOD: (D. gr. 3—8.)
> 1 part Fer: Iod: in 8.
>> Chalybeate Tonic and Alterative.
>>> *Anæmia, Scrofula, Constitutional Syphilis, Cachexia.*

PIL: HYDRARG: (D. gr. 3—8.)
> 1 part Hydrargyrum in 3.
>> Alterative Cathartic.
>>> *Syphilis, Inflammations.*

PIL: HYDRARG: SUBCHLOR: CO: (D. gr. 5—10.)
> 1 part Hydrarg: Subchlor: in 5 parts.
>> Alterative.
>>> *Chronic Skin Affections.*

PIL: IPECAC: c. SCILLÂ: (D. gr. 5—10.)
> Contains 8 parts Pulv: Ipecac: Co: in 7 (1 part Opium in 16¼, nearly).
>> Diaphoretic and Expectorant.

PIL: PLUMB: c. OPIO. (D. gr. 3—5.)
> Acet: Lead, 6 parts; Opium, 1 part; Confect: of Red Roses, 1 part. *N.B.*—Acetate of Morphia and Meconate of Lead are formed in this Pill by double decomposition.
> Useful combination of the two drugs.

PIL: QUINIÆ. (D. gr. 2—10.)
> 8 parts Quinine in 4.
>> Tonic Antiperiodic.
>>> *Intermittent and Remittent Fevers, Neuralgia, Rheumatism.*

PIL: RHEI CO: (D. gr. 5—10.)
> 1 part Aloes in 6; 1 part Rhubarb in 4, nearly.
>> Aperient, slightly Cholagogue.

PIL: SAPONIS CO: (D. gr. 3—5.)
> Contains 1 part Opium in 6, nearly.
>> Narcotic.
>>> *Vide* Opium.

PIL: SCILLÆ CO: (D. gr. 5—10.)
> Contains 1¼ part Scilla and 1 part Ammoniacum in 6, nearly
>> Expectorant, slightly Diuretic.

*PIMENTA.
>AQ: PIMENTÆ, contains ʒxiv to Cj.
>>*Vide* Ol: Pimentæ.

*PIPER NIGRUM.
>Hot and Pungent Stimulant. Febrifuge (?).
>>(Used to prevent the nauseating effects of some m
>>cines, especially Opium.)

PIX BURGUND:
>Preparations:—Emplas: Fer: and Emplas: Picis.
>Slightly Stimulant to the Skin.

PIX LIQUID:
>Alterative Stimulant.
>>*Lepra, Psoriasis, Ichthyosis, and various other Cutan*
>>*Affections; Indolent Ulcers.*
>>>Dose, m. 3—60, in Treacle.
>The vapour is sometimes inhaled in Chronic Bronch

PLUMB: ACET: (D. gr. 1—4.)
>LIQ: PLUMB: SUBACET: contains ʒv to Oj.
>PIL: PLUMB: c. OPIO contains 8 parts in 4.
>SUPPOS: PLUMB: Co: contains 1 part in 5.
>UNG: PLUMB: ACET: contains 1 part in 88.
>>Sedative, Astringent.
>>>*Hæmorrhages, Hæmoptysis, Diarrrhœa, Epileps,*
>>>*Phthisis.*
>>(Should be discontinued when the characteristic
>>line appears on the Gums.)

*PLUMB: CARB:
>UNG: PLUMB: CARB: contains 1 part in 8.
>>EXT: Desiccative, Astringent, Sedative.
>>*Excoriations.*

*PLUMB: IOD:
>EMPLAS: PLUMB: IOD:, contains 1 part in 9.
>UNGT: PLUMB: IOD:, contains 1 part in 8.
>>EXT: Mild Stimulant.
>>>*Scrofulous Swellings. Sometimes given internally.*
>>>Dose, gr. ¼—2.

*PLUMB: NITRAS.
>Used in preparing Plumb: Iod:

*PLUMB: OXID:
>Contained in several preparations.
>>For uses and properties of Lead, *vide* Plumb: Acet:

*PODOPHYL: RAD:
Dose in Powder, gr. 10—20.
Vide Podophyl: Res:

PODOPHYL: RES: (D. gr. ¼—1.)
Drastic Cathartic.
Portal Congestion, Dropsies.

POTAS: CAUST:
LIQ: POTAS:, contains gr. 27 in fl. ʒj.
Powerful Caustic.
Sloughing Ulcers, Carbuncle (after Scalpel). For making Issues.

POTAS: SULPHURAT:
Preparation:—UNG: POTAS: SULPHURAT:
Irritant, Stimulant, Alterative, Diaphoretic.
Dose, gr. 8—15, in form of Pill.

POTAS: ACET: (D. gr. 10—60.)
Diuretic, Cathartic (in doses of ʒj—iij).
Renders the Blood and Secretions Alkaline.
(Appears as Carbonate in the Urine.)

POTAS: BICARB: (D. gr. 10—40.)
20 grs. neutralize { 14 grs. Citric Acid, or
                     15 grs. Tartaric Acid.
LIQ: POTAS: EFFERVES:, contains gr. 80 in Oj.
Antacid, Diuretic.
Acute Rheumatism, Dyspepsia, Uric Acid Deposits.

POTAS: BICHROM:
Employed in making Valerianate of Soda.

POTAS: CARB: (D. gr. 10—80.)
20 grs. neutralize { 17 grs. Citric Acid, or
                     18 grs. Tartaric Acid.
Diuretic, Alterative, Antacid, Antilithic.

POTAS: CHLOR: (D. gr. 10—80.)
TROCH: POTAS: CHLOR:, gr. 5 in each.
Alterative, Refrigerant, Diuretic.
Scarlatina, Typhus, Cholera, Cancrum Oris.

POTAS: CITRAS. (D. gr. 20—60.)
Refrigerant, Diuretic.
Febricula. Uric Acid Diathesis. (Appears in Urine as Carbonate.)

POTAS: NITRAS. (D. gr. 10—80.)
    Refrigerant, Diuretic, Vascular Sedative.
        Dropsy, Scorbutic Affections, Acute Rheumatism.

POTAS: PERMANGAN:
    LIQ: POTAS: PERMANGAN:, contains gr. 4 to fl. ℥j.
    Antiseptic.
        Diabetes (?). Valuable as a Gargle in Malig
          Throat, &c.

*POTAS: PRUSS: FLAV:
    Used in making Acid: Hydrocyan: Dil:

POTAS: SULPH: (D. gr. 15—60.)
    PULV: IPECAC: Co: contains 4 parts in 5.
    Mild Cathartic and Alterative.

POTAS: TART: (D. ℥j—iv.)
    Diuretic and Purgative Saline.
        (Appears as Carbonate in the Urine.)

POTAS: TART: ACID: (D. gr. 20—60.)
    Refrigerant, Diuretic, Hydragogue Cathartic.

POTAS: BROMID: (D. gr. 5—80.)
    Powerful Alterative, Deobstruent, Depressant.
        Chronic Skin Affections. Irritation of Organs o
          tion.
    (Does not produce Coryza.)

POTAS: IOD: (D. gr. 2—10.)
    Preparations :—
    LINIM: IODI, gr. 22 in fl. ℥j, nearly.
    LINIM: POTAS: IOD: c. SAPONE:, gr. 54½ in fl. ℥j, nea
    LIQ: IODI, gr. 80 in fl. ℥j.
    TINCT: IODI, gr. 5½ in fl. ℥j, nearly.
    UNG: IODI, gr. 16 in ℥j, nearly.
    UNG: POTAS: IOD:, 1 part in 8¾, nearly.
        Powerful Alterative. Excitant of the Secretin,
          ting, and Glandular Organs generally. Pre
          Iodine, as it does not irritate the Mucous M
          of Stomach or Intestines.
        Scrofula, Inflammatory Deposits, Hypertrophies,
          Chronic Skin Diseases, Dropsies, Rheumatis
          orrhœa, Leucorrhœa. N.B.—If exhibited too
          duces Iodism.

*PRUNUM.
    Enters into Confect: Sennæ.
        1 part to 12½.

*PTEROCARPI LIG:
    Used in making Tinct: Lavand: Co:

*PULV: AMYGD: CO:
    Mist: Amygd: contains ℥iiฉ to Oj.

PULV: ANTIMON: (D. gr. 8—10.)
    Diaphoretic and Alterative.
        (Less irritating to the Stomach than Tartar Emetic.)

PULV: CATECHU CO: (D. gr. 20—40.)
    Contains 1 part Catechu in 2½.
        Aromatic Astringent.
            Diarrhœa, Atonic Dyspepsia, Hœmorrhages.

PULV: CINNAM: CO: (D. gr. 8—10.)
    Aromatic Stimulant.

PULV: CRETÆ AROMAT: (D. gr. 10—60.)
    Antacid, Astringent, Stimulant.
        Diarrhœa with great Debility.

PULV: CRETÆ AROMAT: c. OPIO. (D. gr. 10—40.)
    Contains 1 part Opium in 40.
        Antacid, Astringent, Stimulant, Narcotic.

PULV: IPECAC: CO: (D. gr. 5—15.)
    Contains 1 part Opium in 10.
      Pil: Ipecac: Co: contains 8 parts in 7.
        Stimulant and Anodyne, Diaphoretic, Nauseant.

PULV: JALAP: CO: (D. gr. 20—60.)
    Hydragogue Cathartic, Vermifuge.
        Habitual Costiveness, Dropsies.
        (Less griping than Jalap.)

PULV: KINO CO: (D. gr. 5—20.)
    Contains 1 part Opium in 20 and 3¾ parts Kino in 5.
        Astringent, Stimulant and Anodyne.

PULV: OPII CO: (D: gr. 2—5.)
    Contains 1 part Opium in 10.
      Confect: Opii contains 1 part in 4, nearly.
      Stimulant, Anodyne.

PULV: RHEI CO: (D. gr. 20—60.)
    Contains 2 parts Rhubarb and 6 parts Light Magnesia in 9.
        Dyspepsia, Diarrhœa.

PULV: SCAM: CO: (D. gr. 10—20.)
4 parts Scam: and 3 parts Jalap in 8.
Cathartic, Anthelmintic.

PULV: TRAGACANTH: CO: (D. gr. 20—60.)
Demulcent.
Principally used as a Vehicle.

*PYRETH: RAD:
TINCT: PYRETH: contains ℥iv to Oj.

*PYROXYLIN.
Vide Collodium and Collodium Flex:

QUASSIÆ LIQ:
INFUS: QUASSIÆ contains gr. 6 to fl. ℥j.
TINCT: QUASSIÆ contains gr. 16½ to fl. ℥j.
Bitter Tonic and Stomachic.

QUERCUS CORT:
Vide Decoct: Quercûs.

QUINIÆ SULPH: (D. gr. 1—10.)
Preparations:—
FER: ET QUINIÆ CITRAS, 16 parts Quinia in 100.
PIL: QUINIÆ, 8 parts in 4.
TINCT: QUINIÆ, gr. 8 in fl. ℥j.
VIN: QUINIÆ, gr. 1 in fl. ℥j.
Tonic, Antiperiodic.
Intermittent and Remittent Fevers, Obstinate Perio
Neuralgia, Rheumatism.

*RESINA.
Mild Stimulant.
Used in many Plasters and Ointments.

*RHAMNI SUC:
Hydragogue Cathartic.
Vide Syr: Rhamni.

RHEI RAD: (D. gr. 5—20.)
Preparations:—
EXT: RHEI.
INFUS: RHEI, gr. 11 to fl. ℥j.
PIL: RHEI Co:, 1 part in 4, nearly.
PULV: RHEI Co:, 2 parts in 9.
SYR: RHEI.
TINCT: RHEI, gr. 44 to fl. ℥j.
VIN: RHEI, gr. 88 to fl. ℥j.
Cathartic, Stomachic, Astringent, and Tonic in sm
doses.

*RHŒAD: PETAL:
   Vide Syr: Rhœad:

*ROSÆ CANIN: FRUCT:
   Vide Confec: Rosæ Canin:

*ROSÆ CENTIFOL: PETAL:
   Vide Aq: Rosæ.

*ROSÆ GALLIC: PETAL:
   Vide Confec: Rosæ Gallic:, Infus: Rosæ Acid:, Syr: Rosæ Gallic:

*SABADILLA.
   Anthelmintic.
     Vide Veratria.

SABINÆ CACUMINA. (D. gr. 4—10, in Powder.)
   Preparations:—
   Ol: Sabinæ.
   Tinct: Sabinæ, ℥ijß dried to Oj.
   Ung: Sabinæ, ℥viij fresh to ℥xix.
     Stimulant, Diuretic, Emmenagogue.

SACCH: PURIF:
   Dietetic, Saccharine Demulcent, Nutrient.
   Used in many preparations to cover nauseous medicines.

SACCH: LACTIS.
   Saccharine Demulcent.
     May be used for same purposes as Sacch: Purif:

*SAMBUC: FLOR:
   Preparation:—Aq: Sambuc:, lb. 10 to Oj.
   Used for flavour and as a Vehicle.

SANTONICA. (D. gr 10—60.)
   Anthelmintic (especially for Lumbricus).

SANTONINUM. (D. gr. 2—6.)
   The active principle of Santonica.

SAPO DUR:
   Emollient, Detergent.
     Mechanically valuable in forming Pills, Plasters, &c.

SAPO MOLL:
   Linim: Terebinth: contains 2 parts in 17½, nearly.
     Emollient, Detergent.
       Mechanically valuable in forming Pills, Plasters, &c.

*SARSÆ RAD:
    Vide Decoct: Sarsæ and Ext: Sarsæ Liquid:

*SASSAFRAS RAO:
    DECOCT: SARSÆ Co:, ʒij to Oj.
      Stimulant, Diaphoretic.

*SCAM: RAD:
    Vide Scam: Res: and Scammonium.

SCAM: RES: (D. gr. 3—8.)
    EXT: COLOCYNTH: Co:, 1 part in 7, nearly.
    MIST: SCAM:, 2 grs. to fl. ʒj.
      Drastic Cathartic.

SCAMMONIUM. (D. gr. 5—10.)
    Preparations:—
    CONFECT: SCAM:, 1 part in 3, nearly.
    PIL: COLOCYNTH: Co:, 1 part in 3, nearly.
    PIL: COLOCYNTH: ET HYOSCYAM:, 1 part in 4½, nearly.
    PULV: SCAM: Co:, 1 part in 2.
    SCAM: RES:
      Drastic Cathartic.

SCILLA. (D. gr. 1—3, in Powder.)
    Preparations:—
    ACET: SCILLÆ, ʒiiꝗ to Oj, nearly.
    OXYMEL SCILLÆ.
    PIL: IPECAC: c. SCILLA, 1 part in 7.
    PIL: SCILLÆ Co:, ʒx to ʒvj, nearly.
    SYR: SCILLÆ.
    TINCT: SCILLÆ, ʒiiꝗ to Oj.
      Expectorant and Diuretic. Cathartic and Emetic in
      large doses.
        Chronic Catarrh, Anasarca with want of power.

*SCOPAR: CACUMIN:
    Vide Decoct: and Suc: Scoparii.

*SENEGÆ: RAO:
    Vide Infus: and Tinct: Senegæ.
      Stimulant and Expectorant. Emetic and Cathartic in
      large doses.

SENNA ALEXAN:
    Preparations:—
    CONFECT: SENNÆ, 1 part in 11, nearly.
    INFUS: SENNÆ, ʒij to Oj.
    MIST: SENNÆ Co:
    SYR: SENNÆ, ʒj to fl. ʒij.
    TINCT: SENNÆ, ʒiiꝗ to Oj.
      Purgative. Chiefly acting on small Intestines.

SENNA IND:
>(May be used as Senna Alexan:)

*SERPENTAR: RAD:
>*Vide* Infus:, Tinct: Serpentar:, and Tinct: Cinch: Co:
>(℥ß to Oj.)
>Stimulant Tonic, Diaphoretic, Diuretic, Emmenagogue.
>>*Atonic Fevers, Exanthemata, Dyspepsia, Chronic Rheumatism.*

*SEVUM: PRÆP:
>Emollient.
>>Used as a basis or adjunct to some Ointments and Plasters.

*SINAPIS.
>*Vide* Cataplas: and Ol: Sinapis.

*SODA CAUST:
>LIQ: SODÆ contains gr. 18·8 in fl. ℥j.

SODA TARTARAT: (D. ℨij—iv.)
>Mild Diuretic and Purgative, Antiphlogistic.
>(Found in the secretions as Carbonate of Soda and Potash.)

SODÆ ACET:
>Diuretic and Cathartic.
>>Dose, ℨj—℥ß.

SODÆ ARSENIAS. (D. gr. $\frac{1}{8}$—$\frac{1}{3}$.)
>Same use as Liq: Arsenicalis and Liq: Arsenici Hydrochlor:
>>LIQ: SODÆ ARSENIATIS contains $\left\{\begin{array}{l}\text{gr. 6·6, or}\\\text{gr. 4 dried}\end{array}\right\}$ in fl. ℥j.

SODÆ BICARB: (D. gr. 10—60.)
>20 grs. neutralize $\left\{\begin{array}{l}\text{16·7 grs. Citric Acid, or}\\\text{17·8 grs. Tartaric Acid.}\end{array}\right.$

>Preparations:—
>LIQ: SODÆ EFFERVES: contains gr. 80 to Oj.
>SODÆ CITRO-TARTRAS EFFERVES: contains 17 parts in 81.
>TROCH: SODÆ BICARB:, gr. 5 in each.
>>Antacid, Diuretic.
>>>*Gastrodynia, Dyspepsia, Gout, &c.*
>>Very similar in action to Bicarbonate of Potash, but not so useful in Uric Acid Diathesis, Urate of Potash being much more soluble than Urate of Soda.

SODÆ CARB: (D. gr. 5—80.)
>28 grs. neutralize $\left\{\begin{array}{l}\text{9·7 grs. Citric Acid, or}\\\text{10·5 grs. Tartaric Acid.}\end{array}\right.$
>>Antacid, Diuretic.
>>>Similar in use to Carbonate of Potash.

SODÆ CARB: EXSIC: (D. gr. 8—10.)
Convenient form where the Anhydrous Salt is wanted,
Pills and Powders.

SODÆ CITRO-TART: EFFERVES: (D. ℨj—iv.)
Cooling Saline Aperient.

*SODÆ NITRAS:
Used in making Arseniate of Soda.

SODÆ PHOSPH: (D. ℨij—ℨj.)
Mild Diuretic and Purgative.
Uric Acid Diathesis.

SODÆ SULPH: (D. ℨij—ℨj.)
Diuretic and Saline Purgative.
(If effloresced the dose must be diminished one-fou

SODÆ VALERIAN: (D. gr. 1—5.)
Antispasmodic.
Vide Valerianæ Radix.

SODII CHLOR:
Alterative, gr. x—ℨj; Emetic, ℨiɴ—ij, in warm wate
Cathartic, ℨɴ—j; for Bath purposes, lb.j to Oiij.
Scrofula, Ague, Malignant Cholera.

SPT: ÆTHERIS. (D. fl. ℨɴ—iɴ.)
Stimulant, Antispasmodic, Anodyne.
Nervous Irritability.

SPT: ÆTHER: NITROS: (D. fl. ℨɴ—ij.)
Stimulant and Antispasmodic, Diaphoretic, Diuretic.
Febrile Affections, Dropsies.
(Applied to the Gums on Cotton Wool in Inflamma

SPT: AMMON: AROMAT: (D. fl. ℨɴ—j.)
Aromatic Diffusible Stimulant, Antacid, Antispasmodic
Syncope, Hysteria, Pneumonia, Bronchitis, Low Fev

SPT: AMMON: FŒTID: (D. fl. ℨɴ—j.)
Stimulant, Antispasmodic, Expectorant.
Hysteria, Pertussis, Asthma, Bronchitis.

SPT: ARMORAC: CO: (D. fl. ℨj—ij.)
Stimulant, Sudorific.
Atonic Dyspepsia, Chronic Rheumatism.

SPT: CAJUPUTI. (D. fl. ℨɴ—j.)
Stimulant and Antispasmodic.
Colic, Hysteria, Cholera, Rheumatism.

SPT: CAMPH: (D. m. 10—30.)
  Stimulant, and then Sedative; Antispasmodic, Diaphoretic.
    Dysmenorrhœa, Rheumatism, Febricula.

SPT: CHLOROFORM: (D. m. 20—60.)
  Contains 1 vol. of Chloroform in 20.
    Narcotic and Antispasmodic. Stimulant, Cordial, Antiperiodic (?).
      Asthma, Cholera, Hysteria, Lead Colic, Neuralgia, Cancer, &c.

SPT: JUNIPER: (D. fl. ʒꬱ—j.)
  Contained in Mist: Creasoti.
    Stimulant and Diuretic.
      Dropsies.

SPT: LAVAND: (D. fl. ʒꬱ—j.)
  Stimulant, Carminative.
    Hysteria, Hypochondriasis, Flatulence, Colic.

SPT: MENTH: PIP: (D. fl. ʒꬱ—j.)
  Stimulant, Carminative.
  Corrects Flatulency.

SPT: MYRIST: (D. fl. ʒꬱ—j.)
  Contained in Mist: Fer: Co:
    Aromatic, gently Stimulant, slightly Narcotic. Useful also as a Flavouring Agent.

*SPT: RECTIF: (Sp. Gr. 0·838.)
  Diffusible Stimulant.
    The Tinctures marked (s.r.) are made with Rectified Spirit.

SPT: ROSMAR:
  Stimulant, Carminative.
    An elegant adjunct to Lotions and Liniments.

SPT: TENUIOR. (Sp. Gr. 0·920.)
  Excepting Tinct: Guaiaci Ammoniat:, Tinct: Lobeliæ, Æth:, and Tinct: Valerian: Ammoniat:, all the Tinctures not marked (s.r.) are made with Proof Spirit.

SPT: VINI GALLIC:
  Preparation:—MIST: SPT: VINI GALLIC:
  Powerful Diffusible Stimulant.

STRAMON: FOLIA.
  Cautiously smoked in Spasmodic Asthma it frequently gives relief.

*STRAMON: SEM:
Vide Ext: and Tinct: Stramonii, (54¼ grs. to fl. ʒj.)
Anodyne, Antispasmodic.

STRYCHNIA. (D. gr. $\frac{1}{30}$—$\frac{1}{12}$.)
LIQ: STRYCHNIÆ contains ½ gr. in fl. ʒj.
Stimulant to Spinal Cord, Bitter Stomachic, Tonic, A
periodic (?).
Paralysis, Dyspepsia.

STYRAX PRÆP:
TINCT: BENZOIN: Co: contains gr. 88 to fl. ʒj.
Stimulant, Expectorant.
Dose, 3ß—j.

SUC: CONII. (D. fl. 3ß—j.)
Vide Conii Folia.
Deobstruent, Alterative, Antispasmodic, Anodyne
Hypnotic.
Cancer, Scrofula, Pertussis, Tetanus.

SUC: SCOPARII. (D. fl. ʒj—ij.)
Diuretic.
Dropsies depending on Heart Disease.

SUC: TARAX: D. fl. ʒj—ij.)
Aperient, Deobstruent, Alterative.
Chronic Liver and Cutaneous Diseases.

SULPH: PRÆCIP: (D. grs. 20—60.)
Diaphoretic and Alterative in small doses. Laxativ
Cathartic in larger doses.

SULPH: SUBLIM: (D. grs. 20—60.)
(Purer than Sulph: Præcip:, which see.)
CONFECT: SULPH: contains 4 parts in 10, nearly.
UNG: SULPH:, 1 part in 5.

SULPH: IOD:
UNG: SULPH: IOD: contains 80 grs. in ʒj.
Acts similarly to Iodine.
EXT: Porrigo-Lepra, Acne, Scabies.
(May be given internally in doses from gr. ¼—

*SUMBUL RAD:
Vide Tinct: Sumbul. (gr. 54¼ in fl. ʒj.)

SUPPOS: ACID: TANNIC:
Gr. 8 Tannic Acid in each.
After irritating and frequent motions.

SUPPOS: HYDRARG:
Gr. 5 Ointment of Mercury in each.
> *Thread-worms, Syphilitic and other Sores in Rectum (or Vagina.)*

SUPPOS: MORPHIÆ.
Gr. ⅛ of Hydrochlorate of Morphia in each.
> May be used either for the local or general effects of Morphia.

SUPPOS: PLUMB: CO:
Gr. j of Opium and gr. 8 of Acetate of Lead in each.
> *Painful Ulcers about the Rectum.*

SYRUPUS.
Refined Sugar, lbv; Distilled Water, Oij.
> Saccharine Demulcent, Dietetic, Nutrient.
>> Useful as a Vehicle and pleasant Adjunct. Enters into many Pharmaceutical Compounds.

SYR: AURANT: (D. fl. ℥j.)
Contained in Confect: Sulph:
> Aromatic, Bitter Stomachic.

SYR: AURANT: FLOR: (D. fl. ℥j.)
Vehicle for Flavour.

SYR: FER: IOD: (D. fl. ℥ß—j.)
Contains 4·8 grs. Fer: Iod: in fl. ℥j.
> Chalybeate Tonic and Alterative.
>> *Anæmia, Scrofula, Cachexia.*

SYR: FER: PHOSPH: (D. fl. ℥j.)
Valuable Nervine and Blood Tonic.
> *Diabetes, Rickets, Anæmia, Cachexia.*

SYR: HEMIDESMI. (D. fl. ℥j.)
Vide Hemidesmi Rad:

SYR: LIMON: (D. fl. ℥j.)
1 pint Limon Suc: to 8½ pounds.
> Acidulous Refrigerant.

SYR: MORI. (D. fl. ℥j.)
A Colouring Agent.

SYR: PAPAVER: (D. fl. ℥j.)
Anodyne and Narcotic.

SYR: RHAMNI. (D. fl. ℥j.)
Hydragogue Cathartic. Liable to Nauseate and Gripe.
(Mostly used for Children.)

SYR: RHEI. (D. fl. 3j—iv.)
Cordial Purgative.

SYR: RHŒAD: (D. fl. 3j.)
A Colouring Agent. Slightly Narcotic (?).

SYR: ROSÆ GALLIC: (D. fl. 3j.)
Slightly Astringent.
(Used for Colouring and Flavouring.)

SYR: SCILLÆ. (D. 3a—j.)
Expectorant. Sometimes used as an Emetic for Childre

SYR: SENNÆ. (D. fl. 3j—iv.)
Mild Purgative.

SYR: TOLUT: (D. fl. 3j.)
Stimulant, Expectorant.

SYR: ZINGIB: (D. fl. 3j.)
Warm and pleasant Adjunct to Medicines.

TABACI FOLIA.
ENEMA TABACI contains Əj to fl. ℥viij boiling water.
Sedative, Antispasmodic, Laxative, Diuretic, Em
As commonly used, Stimulant, Errhine and Sialogo
Valuable in reducing Muscular Spasm in case
Strangulated Hernia.

TAMARINDUS.
CONFECT: SENNÆ contains 9 parts in 75.
Refrigerant, Laxative.

TARAX: RAD:
Vide Decoct: (℥j to Oj), Ext: and Suc: Tarax:

TEREBINTH: CANAD: (D. gr. 20—30.)
Antispasmodic and Astringent.
EXT: Stimulant, Rubefacient.

THERIACA.
Slightly Laxative.
Chiefly used in administering Pix Liquida, Sulphur,
and to give consistence to Pills.

THUS AMERIC:
Mild Stimulant.
Preparation :—EMPLAS: PICIS.

(s.R.) TINCT: ACONITI. (D. m. 5—15.)
Anodyne and Diuretic.
Rheumatism, Gout, Neuralgia, Cancer, Heart Dise
Dropsies.

TINCT: ALOE: (D. fl. 3j—ij.)
 11 grs. Aloe: Soc: in fl. 3j.
  Cathartic.

(s.b.) **TINCT: ARNICÆ.** (D. fl. 3j—ij.)
 INT: Stimulant and Irritant.
 EXT: Discussive.
  Ecchymosis, Bruises, Sprains.

(s.b.) **TINCT: ASSAFŒT:** (D. fl. 3ꝰ—j.)
 Stimulant, Powerful Antispasmodic, Expectorant.
  In Hysteria, Pertussis, Asthma, Bronchitis.

TINCT: AURANT: (D. fl. 3j—ij.)
 Stomachic Tonic.
 Preparations:—
  MIST: FER: AROMAT: contains 1 vol. in 32.
  SYR: AURANT:, 1 vol. in 8.
  TINCT: QUINÆ.

TINCT: BELLADON: (D. m. 5—20.)
 Anodyne and Antispasmodic.
  Neuralgia, Gastrodynia, Chorea, Epilepsy, Hysteria, Asthma, &c.

(s.b.) **TINCT: BENZOIN: CO:** (D. fl. 3ꝰ—j.)
 Stimulant, Expectorant.
  EXT: Stimulant to Ulcers and Wounds.

TINCT: BUCHU. (D. fl. 3j—ij.)
 Stimulant, Tonic, Diuretic, Diaphoretic.
  Catarrh of Urinary Organs.

TINCT: CALUMB: (D. fl. 3ꝰ—ij.)
 Bitter Stomachic and Tonic.

TINCT: CAMPH: CO: (D. m. 15—fl. 3j.)
 Contains 2 grs. each of Opium and Benzoic Acid, and gr. 1½
  of Camphor to fl. 3j.
   Valuable as an Opiate, without the debilitating effects of
    the drug. One of the best forms for administering
    Opium to Children. Especially useful in allaying
    irritation in the air passages.
   *Troublesome Coughs, Diarrhœa, Sleeplessness. Useful in
    almost any case where Opium is indicated.*

(s.b.) **TINCT: CANNAB: IND:** (D. m. 5—20.)
 Antispasmodic, Anodyne, Hypnotic.
  Tetanus, Cough, Cramp.

TINCT: CANTHAR: (D. m. 5—20.)
Stimulant, Diuretic.
> INT: Incontinence of Urine, Gleet, Leucorrhœa.
> EXT: Rubefacient.

(S.R.) TINCT: CAPSICI. (D. m. 10—20.)
Irritant, Stimulant.
> Diluted, as a Gargle for Relaxed Sore Throat.

TINCT: CARDAM: CO: (D. fl. 3ʒ—ij.)
Preparations :—
DECOCT: ALOES Co:, 1 vol. in 8¾.
MIST: FER: AROMAT:, 8 vols. in 16.
MIST: SENNÆ Co:, 1 vol. in 16.
TINCT: CHLOROFORMI Co:, 1 vol. in 2.
> Aromatic Adjunct to Draughts, &c.

TINCT: CASCARIL: (D. fl. 3ʒ—ij.)
Stimulant and Warm Tonic, Febrifuge (?).
> *Dyspepsia.*

(S.R.) TINCT: CASTOR: (D. fl. 3ʒ—j.)
Slightly Stimulant and Antispasmodic.

TINCT: CATECHU: (D. fl. 3ʒ—ij.)
Strongly Astringent.
> *Diarrhœa, Atonic Dyspepsia, Hæmorrhages.*

TINCT: CHIRATÆ. (D. fl. 3ʒ—ij.
Bitter Tonic in Convalescence, Stomachic in Dyspepsia.

TINCT: CHLOROFORM: CO: (D. m. 20—60.)
Contains 1 vol. of Chloroform in 10.
> Narcotic and Antispasmodic, Stimulant Cordial.
> *Lead Colic, Hysteria.*

TINCT: CINCH: CO: (D. fl. 3ʒ—ij.)
Stimulant Tonic, Antiperiodic.

TINCT: CINCH: FLAV: (D. fl. 3ʒ—ij.)
Tonic, Antiperiodic.

TINCT: CINNAM: (D. fl. 3ʒ—ij.)
Grateful adjunct where a Stomachic and gentle Stimulat
are required.

TINCT: COCCI.
For Colouring only.

TINCT: COLCH: SEM: (D. m. 10—80.)
Vide Colch: Corm:

TINCT: CONII. (D. m. 20—60.)
Anodyne, Hypnotic, Deobstruent, Alterative, Antispasmodic.
Scrofula, Cancer, Pertussis, Tetanus, Glandular Enlargements.

TINCT: CROCI.
Slightly Stimulant. (May be given in doses of fl. ℥ss—ij.)
Exanthemata. (Chiefly used for Colouring.)

(S.B.) TINCT: CUBEBÆ. (D. fl. ℥ss—ij.)
Stimulant (especially on Urinary Organs).
Gonorrhœa, Gleet.

TINCT: DIGITALIS. (D. m. 10—80.)
Indirectly Sedative, Diuretic.
Heart Disease, Fevers, Inflammations, Dropsies, Pulmonary Affections, Nervous Irritability.

TINCT: ERGOT: (D. m. 10—fl. ℥j.)
fl. ℥j contains gr. 109 of Ergot.
General Astringent and Emmenagogue
In protracted Labour from want of Uterine power.

(S.B.) TINCT: FER: ACET: (D. m. 5—30.)
An agreeable Chalybeate Tonic. (Liable to decompose.)

(S.B.) TINCT: FER: PERCHLOR: (D. m. 10—80.)
Strongly Astringent Ferruginous Tonic, Diuretic.
Anœmia, Passive Hœmorrhage.

TINCT: GALLÆ. (D. fl. ℥ss—ij.)
Astringent.
Vide Acid: Gallic: and Acid: Tannic:

TINCT: GENTIAN: CO: (D. fl. ℥ss—ij.)
Tonic Stomachic.
Atonic Dyspepsia. In convalescence after acute complaints.

TINCT: GUAIACI AMMONIAT: (D. fl. ℥ss—j.)
Vide Guaiaci Res:
Especially useful in Chronic Rheumatism.

TINCT: HYOSCYAMI. (D. fl. ℥ss—j.)
Narcotic, Anodyne, Soporific.
(Does not constipate the Bowels.)

(S.B.) TINCT: IODI. (D. m. 5—20.)
Preparation :—VAPOR IODI.
Alterative, Absorbent, Diuretic.
Syphilis, Scrofula, Chronic Glandular Enlargements.

TINCT: JALAP: (D. fl. 3ꝶ—ij.)
Hydragogue Cathartic.
(Should be given with some Aromatic.)

(s.b.) TINCT: KINO. (D. fl. 3ꝶ—ij.)
Powerful Astringent.

TINCT: KRAMERIÆ. (D. fl. 3ꝶ—ij.)
Astringent Tonic.

(s.b.) TINCT: LAVAND: CO: (D. fl. 3ꝶ—ij.)
Stimulant Cordial, Aromatic. (Used for Colouring Liquor
Arsenicalis.)
Hysteria, Flatulent Colic.

TINCT: LIMON: (D. fl. 3ꝶ—ij.)
Aromatic and Tonic.

TINCT: LOBELIÆ. (D. m. 10—80.)
Expectorant and Diaphoretic, Emetic and Cathartic in large
doses.
Spasmodic Asthma.

TINCT: LOBELIÆ ÆTH: (D. m. 10—80.)
Vide Tinct: Lobeliæ.

TINCT: LUPULI. (D. 3ꝶ—ij.)
Tonic, Stomachic, slightly Narcotic.

(s.b.) TINCT: MYRRH: (D. fl. 3ꝶ—j.)
Stomachic, Stimulant, Expectorant, Antispasmodic.
Emmenagogue.
Ext: as a Stimulant to Ulcers.

TINCT: NUCIS VOMICÆ. (D. m. 10—20.)
Contains 44 grs. in fl. ʒj.
Powerful Excitant of the Spinal Cord; Bitter Stomachic,
Tonic, Antiperiodic (?).

TINCT: OPII. (D. m. 5—40.)
Contains 88 grs. to fl. ʒj, nearly.
Powerfully Anodyne and Narcotic.
Vide Opium.

(s.b.) TINCT: OPII AMMONIAT: (D. fl. 3ꝶ—j.)
Contains 5 grs. to fl. ʒj.
Similar in action to Tinct: Camph: Co:, but contains
2½ times as much Opium.

(s.b.) TINCT: PYRETH:
Irritant Sialogogue.
Local Application in Tooth-ache.

TINCT: QUASSIÆ. (D. fl. ʒꝶ—ij.)
Bitter Tonic and Stomachic, Antiperiodic.
Indigestion from Gout, Alcoholism, &c.

TINCT: QUINIÆ. (D. fl. ʒꝶ—ij.)
Tonic Antiperiodic.
Intermittent and Remittent Fevers; Obstinate Periodic Neuralgia, Rheumatism.

TINCT: RHEI. ⎰ D. (Stomachic, fl. ʒj—ij.)
⎱ (Purgative, fl. ʒꝶ—j.)
Contains grs. 44 in fl. ʒj.
Cordial Stomachic, Purgative.

TINCT: SABINÆ. (D. m. 20—60.)
Stimulant, Diuretic, Emmenagogue.

TINCT: SCILLÆ. (D. m. 10—80.)
Expectorant and Diuretic.
Chronic Catarrh, Anasarca from want of power.

TINCT: SENEGÆ. (D. fl. ʒꝶ—ij.)
Stimulant, Sialogogue, Expectorant, Diaphoretic, Diuretic, Emmenagogue.

TINCT: SENNÆ. (D. fl. ʒj—iv.)
MIST: SENNÆ Co: contains fl. ʒj in fl. ʒj.
Warm and Stimulating Purgative.

TINCT: SERPENTAR: (D. fl. ʒꝶ—ij.)
Stimulant, Diaphoretic, Tonic, Emmenagogue.

TINCT: STRAMON: (D. m. 10—80.)
Anodyne, Antispasmodic.
(Acts similar to Belladonna.)
Neuralgia, Rheumatism, Mania.

TINCT: SUMBUL. (D. m. 10—80.)
Stimulant, Antispasmodic.
Typhoid Fever, Delirium Tremens, Asthma, Hysteria, Epilepsy.

(s.r.) TINCT: TOLUT: (D. m. 20—40.)
Enters into several Lozenges.
Stimulant, Expectorant.
Chronic Bronchitis, Rheumatism, Gleet, Leucorrhœa.

TINCT: VALERIAN: (D. fl. ʒj—ij.)
Stimulant, Antispasmodic.
Hysteria, Globus, Palpitation, Chorea, Epilepsy,

TINCT: VALERIAN: AMMONIAT: (D. fl. 3ß—j.)
More stimulating than the simple Tincture.

(s.b.) TINCT: VERATRI VIR: (D. m. 5—20.)
Vascular Depressant, Purgative (?).
Gout, Rheumatism, Neuralgia.

(s.b.) TINCT: ZINGIB: (D. m. 15—60.)
Warm Aromatic Stomachic.
Atonic Dyspepsia, Flatulence.

(s.b.) TINCT: ZINGIB: FORT: (D. m. 5—20.)
Enters into Syr: Zingib: (fl. 3vj in Oj.)

*TRAGACANTHA.
Mucilaginous Demulcent.   Used principally as a Vehicle.

TROCH: ACID: TANNIC: (D. 1 to 6 Lozenges.)
TANNIC ACID, gr. ½ in each.
Relaxed Throat, Hoarseness.

TROCH: BISMUTH: (D. 1 to 6 Lozenges.)
SUBNITRATE OF BISMUTH, gr. 2 in each.
Sedative to Mucous Membrane of Alimentary Canal.

TROCH: CATECHU. (D. 1 to 6 Lozenges.)
CATECHU, gr. 1 in each.
Moderately strong Astringent.
Relaxed Throat, Hoarseness.

TROCH: FER: REDACT: (D. 1 to 6 Lozenges.)
REDUCED IRON, gr. 1 in each.
In Relaxed Throat, where Iron may be desirable.

TROCH: IPECAC: (D. 1 to 8 Lozenges.)
IPECACUANHA, ¼ gr. in each.
Expectorant and Diaphoretic.

TROCH: MORPHIÆ. (D. 1 to 6 Lozenges.)
HYDROCHLORATE OF MORPHIA, gr. $\frac{1}{36}$ in each.
Allays troublesome Coughing.

TROCH: MORPHIÆ ET IPECAC: (D. 1 to 6 Lozenges.)
Contains $\frac{1}{36}$ g. MORPHIÆ HYDROCHLOR: and $\frac{1}{12}$ gr. IPECAC:
Anodyne, Expectorant, and Diaphoretic.

TROCH: OPII. (D. 1 to 6 Lozenges.)
EXTRACT OF OPIUM, gr. $\frac{1}{10}$ in each.
Anodyne, Hypnotic, allays Cough.

CH: POTAS: CHLOR: (D. 1 to 6 Lozenges.)
CHLORATE OF POTASH, gr. 5 in each.

Sore Throat, Scarlatina.

CH: SODÆ BICARB: (D. 1 to 6 Lozenges.)
BICARBONATE OF SODA, gr. 5 in each.

Antacid.

Gastrodynia, Dyspepsia.

CORT:
Vide Decoct: Ulmi.

: ACONITIÆ.
ACONITIA, gr. 8 to ℨj, nearly.

Directly Sedative to the Nerves of Sensation.

Tic-Doloreux and other forms of Neuralgia; Chronic Rheumatic Pains.

: ANTIMON: TARTARAT:
1 part in 5.

Powerful Counter-Irritant.

Diseased Joints, Inflammations of a Chronic nature.

: ATROPIÆ.
ATROPIÆ, gr. 8 in ℨj.

Anodyne. (Dilates the Pupil locally applied.)

Neuralgia, Spasmodic Contraction of Urethra.

: BELLADON:
EXT: BELLADONNÆ, ℈iv to Prepared Lard ℨj.

Anodyne. (Dilates the Pupil locally applied.)

Neuralgia, Spasmodic Contraction of Urethra.

: CADMII IOD:
Gr. 62 to Simple Ointment ℨj.

Acts like Ung: Plumb: Iod:, but without staining.

: CANTHAR:
1 part in 8.

Irritant and Vesicant.

: CETACEI.
Spermaceti ℨv, White Wax ℨij, Almond Oil Oj or q.s.

Emollient Dressing.

: CREASOTI.
1 part in 9.

Stimulant, Antiseptic

Chronic Skin Disorders.

UNG: ELEMI.
ELEMI, 1 part in 5.
Stimulant.
(Acts like other Turpentines.)

UNG: GALLÆ.
Powdered Galls Ꝝiv. to Benzoated Lard ℥j.
Astringent.
External Hæmorrhoids.

UNG: GALLÆ c. OPIO.
32 grs. of Opium to ℥j.
Astringent and Anodyne.
External Hæmorrhoids.

UNG: HYDRARG:
1 part Mercury in 2 parts.
Alterative. (Acts on the system, when abs
Mercury given internally.)
Syphilitic Sores.

UNG: HYDRARG: AMMONIAT:
Gr. 62 to ℥j.
Stimulant, Alterative.
Pediculi, Chronic Skin Diseases.

UNG: HYDRARG: CO:
1 part Mercury in 4½.
Alterative, Absorbent.
Various Diseases of Joints.

UNG: HYDRARG: IOD: RUB:
1 part in 28.
Stimulant, Absorbent.
Goitre, Enlarged Glands, Nodes.

UNG: HYDRARG: NITRAT:
Stimulant, Alterative.
Inflammatory Diseases of the Eye, Skin Affecti

UNG: HYDRARG: OXID: RUB:
Gr. 62 to ℥j.
Stimulant, Absorbent.
Indolent Sores, Chronic Ophthalmia.

UNG: HYDRARG: SUBCHLOR:
Ꝝiv to ℥j.
Alterative, Absorbent.
Chronic Skin Affections.

UNG: IODI.
>Iodine and Iodide of Potassium 16 grs. each to 3j.
>A good form for external application of Iodine.

UNG: PICIS LIQUID:
>Tar, fl 3v, Yellow Wax, 3ij.
>>Stimulant.
>>>*Porrigo, Lepra and other Skin Diseases, Indolent Ulcers.*

UNG: PLUMB: ACET:
>Gr. 12 to Benzoated Lard 3j.
>>*Cooling and Soothing to Burns, Blisters, Irritable Sores, &c.*

UNG: PLUMB: CARB:
>Gr. 62 to 3j.
>>*Cooling and Drying to Irritable Burns, Ulcers, Eruptions, &c.*

UNG: PLUMB: IOD:
>Gr. 62 to 3j.
>>Mild Stimulant, Discutient.
>>>*Scrofulous Enlargement of Joints.*

UNG: PLUMB: SUBACET: CO:
>Sedative, Soothing, Astringent.
>>*Irritable Ulcers, &c. Chronic Ophthalmia.*

UNG: POTAS: SULPHURAT:
>Gr. 30 to 3j.
>>Detergent.
>>>*Scabies, Psoriasis, Chronic Rheumatism.*
>(When used should be freshly prepared.)

UNG: POTAS: IOD:
>Gr. 64 to 3j, nearly.
>>Slowly produces the effects of Iodine without the irritation.

UNG: RESINÆ.
>Resin 3ij, Yellow Wax 3j, Simple Ointment 3iv.
>>Stimulant.
>>>*Indolent Sores.*

UNG: SABINÆ.
>Used to keep open Blisters and Setons.

UNG: SIMPLEX.
>White Wax 3ij, Prepared Lard 3iij, Almond Oil fl. 3iij.
>>Enters into several Ointments.

UNG: SULPH:

Sublimed Sulphur ℨi, Benzoated Lard ℥iv.

Alterative.

Scabies and other Skin Affections.

UNG: SULPH: IOD:

Gr. 80 to ℥j.

Alterative. Acts like Iodine.

Porrigo, Lepra, Acne, Scabies, &c.

UNG: TEREBINTH:

OIL OF TURPENTINE, 1 part in 2, nearly.

Stimulant.

Foul and Indolent Ulcers.

UNG: VERATRIÆ.

Gr. 8 to ℥j, nearly.

Scabies, some Chronic Skin Affections, Neuralgia, Rheuma tism, Gout.

UNG: ZINCI.

Oxide of Zinc Əiv to Benzoated Lard ℥j.

Desiccative and slightly Astringent.

*UVÆ URSI FOLIA.

Vide Infus: Uvæ Ursi. (℥j to Oj.)

Astringent Tonic, Diuretic.

*UVÆ.

Saccharine Demulcent.

Enters into Tinct: Cardam: Co: and Tinct: Sennæ.

VALERIANÆ RAD: (D. gr. 10—80.)

Diffusible Stimulant and Antispasmodic.

Vide Infus: and Tinct: Valerian:, and Tinct: Valerian Ammoniat

†VAPOR ACID: HYDROCYAN:

Dilute Hydrocyanic Acid, m. 10 to 15; Water (cold), fl. 3 Mix, and inhale the vapour.

†VAPOR CHLORI.

Chlorinated Lime, ℥ij; Water (cold,) q.s. Moisten the Pow der with the water and inhale the vapour.

†VAPOR CONIÆ.

Extract of Hemlock, 3j; Solution of Potash, fl. 3j; Distille Water, fl. 3x. Mix. Moisten a sponge with 20 drops an inhale the vapour of hot water passing over and through

---

† In each case a suitable Apparatus or Inhaler must be employed.

POR CREASOTI.
Creasote, m. 12; Boiling Water, fl. ℥viij. Mix, and inhale the vapour, together with air, made to pass through the solution.
Stimulant, Antiseptic.

Chronic Bronchitis, Pulmonary Abscess, Fœtid Breath.

POR IODI.
Tincture of Iodine, fl. ʒj; Water, fl. ℥j. Mix. Apply gentle heat and inhale the vapour.

Chronic Bronchitis, Phthisis.

RATRI VIR: RAD:
Preparation:—TINCT: VERATRI VIR:, ℥iv to Oj.
Vascular Depressant, Purgative (?).

Gout, Rheumatism, Neuralgia.

RATRIA.
Preparation:—UNG: VERATRIÆ, gr. 8 to ℥j.
Anthelmintic, Nauseant, Emetic, Purgative.

(Dose, gr. $\frac{1}{12}$—$\frac{1}{6}$).

Gout, Rheumatism.

N: ALOE: (D. fl. ʒj—ij.)
Gr. 16½ in fl. ℥j.
Warm Cathartic, Emmenagogue. In small doses Tonic and Stomachic.

N: ANTIMON: (D. m. 5—60.)
Diaphoretic, Expectorant, Cholagogue, Emetic, Purgative, Vascular Depressant.

N: AURANT:
Used in Vin: Fer: Citrat: and Vin: Quiniæ.

N: COLCH: (D. m. 10—80.)
Vide Colch: Corm:

N: FER: (D. fl. ʒj—iv.)
Mild Stimulant Tonic.

IN: FER: CITRAT: (D. fl. ʒj—iv.)
Gr. 8 to fl. ℥j.
Mild Ferruginous Tonic. (Not Astringent nor Irritant.)

IN: IPECAC: { D. (m. 5—40, Expectorant.) (fl. ʒiij—vi, Emetic.)
Gr. 22 in fl. ℥j.
Vide Ipecacuanha.

---

† In each case a suitable Apparatus or Inhaler must be employed.

VIN: OPII. (D. m. 10—40.)
Contains gr. 22 Ext: Opii to fl. ℥j, nearly.
Vide Opium.

VIN: QUINIÆ. (D. fl. ℥ss—j.)
Gr. 1 to fl. ℥j.
Elegant form for exhibiting Quinine.

VIN: RHEI. (D. fl. ℥j—ij.)
Contains 88 grs. in fl. ℥j.
Stomachic and Purgative.

VIN: XERIC:
Stimulant. (More apt to turn acid than Brandy.)

ZINCI ACETAS. { D. (Tonic, gr. 1—2.) (Emetic, gr. 10—20.)
Ext: Astringent.
Int: Tonic, Antispasmodic.
Hysteria, Epilepsy.

*ZINCI CARB:
Desiccative (similar in action to Oxide of Zinc).
Excoriations, &c.

*ZINCI CHLOR:
Ext: Powerful Escharotic.
Liq: Zinci Chlor: contains gr. 866 in fl. ℥j.
Mixed with Plaster of Paris it is sometimes applied as a paste to Venereal Warts, &c.

ZINCI OXID: (D. gr. 2—10.)
Preparation:—Ung: Zinci, 1 part in 6½, nearly.
Ext: Absorbent, Desiccant.
Int: Tonic Antispasmodic.

ZINCI SULPH: { D. (Tonic, gr. 1—3.) (Emetic, gr. 10—30.)
Ext: Astringent (in Solution).
Int: Astringent, Antispasmodic, Emetic.
Epilepsy, Hysteria, Gonorrhœa.

ZINCI VALERIAN: (D: gr. 1—3.)
Antispasmodic, Nervine Tonic.
Chorea, Epilepsy, Neuralgia, Anthelmintic (?).

*ZINCUM.
Vide Preparations of Zinc.

*ZINCUM GRANULAT:
    Used in making Liq : Zinci Chlor :, Zinci Chlor :, and Zinci
    Sulph :

ZINGIBER.
    Pleasant warm Aromatic, Rubefacient, Errhine, Sialogogue,
    Stimulant Stomachic.
        Atonic Dyspepsia, Flatulence.   *Corrects the griping of
        various Purgatives.*
    Used in many Preparations.

WEIGHTS AND MEASURES OF THE
BRITISH PHARMACOPŒIA.

WEIGHTS.

1 Grain	gr.		
(20 grains	=	Ɖ)	
(60 grains	=	Ʒ)	
1 Ounce	oz. (Ʒ)	=	437·5 grains
1 Pound	lb. = 16 ounces	=	7000 „

MEASURES OF CAPACITY.

1 Minim	min.		
1 Fluid Drachm	fl. drm. (fl. Ʒ)	=	60 minims
1 Fluid Ounce	fl. oz. (fl. Ʒ)	=	8 fluid drachɱ
1 Pint	O.	=	20 fluid ounɱ
1 Gallon	C.	=	8 pints

MEASURES OF LENGTH.

1 line $= \frac{1}{12}$ inch

1 inch $= \frac{1}{39.1393}$ seconds pendulum

12 „ $=$ 1 foot

36 „ $=$ 3 „ $=$ 1 yard

Length of Pendulum vibrating seconds of mean time in the latitude of London, in a vacuum at the level of the sea . . . } 39·1393 inch

RELATION OF MEASURES TO WEIGHTS.

1 Minim is the measure of		0·91 grains of
1 Fluid Drachm „		54·68	„
1 Fluid Ounce „	1 ounce or	437·5	„
1 Pint „	1·25 pounds or 8750·0		„
1 Gallon „	10 pounds or 70,000·0		„

WEIGHTS AND MEASURES OF THE METRICAL SYSTEM.

WEIGHTS.

Milligramme = the thousandth part of one grm. or 0·001 grm.
Centigramme = the hundredth   ,,   0·01 ,,
Decigramme = the tenth   ,,   0·1 ,,
Gramme = weight of a cubic centimetre of   1·0 ,,
        water at 4° C.
Decagramme = ten grammes   ,,   10·0 ,,
Hectogramme = one hundred grammes ,,   100·0 ,,
Kilogramme = one thousand grammes ,,   1000·0 ,,

MEASURES OF CAPACITY.

Millilitre =   1 cub. centim. or the mea. of 1 gram. of water
Centilitre =   10   ,,   10 ,,   ,,
Decilitre =   100   ,,   100 ,,   ,,
Litre = 1000   ,,   1000 ,, (1 kilo.)

MEASURES OF LENGTH.

Millimetre = the thousandth part of one metre or 0·001 metre
Centimetre = the hundredth   ,,   0·01 ,,
Decimetre = the tenth part   ,,   0·1 ,,
Metre = the ten millionth part of a quarter of the
        meridian of the earth.

RELATION OF THE WEIGHTS OF THE BRITISH PHARMACOPŒIA TO THE METRICAL WEIGHTS.

1 Pound	=	453·5925 grammes
1 Ounce	=	28·3495 ,,
1 Grain	=	0·0648 ,,

RELATION OF MEASURES OF CAPACITY OF THE BRITISH PHARMACOPŒIA TO THE METRICAL MEASURES.

1 Gallon	=	4·543487 litres		
1 Pint	=	0·567936 ,,	or 567·936 cubic centimetres	
1 Fluid Ounce	=	0·028396 ,,	28·396	,,
1 Fluid Drachm	=	0·003549 ,,	3·549	,,
1 Minim	=	0·000059 ,,	0·059	,,

RELATION OF THE METRICAL WEIGHTS TO THE WEIGHTS OF THE BRITISH PHARMACOPŒIA.

1 Milligramme	=	0·015432 grs.
1 Centigramme	=	0·15432 ,,
1 Decigramme	=	1·5432 ,,
1 Gramme	=	15·432 ,,
1 Kilogramme	= 2 lbs. 3 oz. 119·8 grs, or 15432·348	,,

RELATION OF THE METRICAL MEASURES TO THE MEASURES OF THE BRITISH PHARMACOPŒIA.

1 Millimetre	=	0·00937 inches
1 Centimetre	=	0·39371 ,,
1 Decimetre	=	3·93708 ,,
1 Metre	=	39·37079 ,, or 1 yard 3·7 inches
1 Cubic Centimetre	=	15·432 grain-measures
1 Litre = 1 pint 15 oz. 2 drs. 11 m. or 15432·348 grain-measures